Kidnapped

Robert L. Stevenson

Published by Priory Books, Bridlington.
A Peter Haddock Limited imprint.
© B. W. (Leicester) Limited.

CHAPTER I

I SET OFF UPON MY JOURNEY
TO THE HOUSE OF SHAWS

I will begin the story of my adventures with a certain
morning early in the month of June, the year of grace 1751,
when I took the key for the last time out of the door of
my father's house. The sun began to shine upon the summit
of the hills as I went down the road; and by the time I had
come as far as the manse, the blackbirds were whistling in
the garden lilacs.

Mr. Campbell, the minister of Essendean, was waiting for
me by the garden gate, good man !

"Well, Davie, lad," said he, "I will go with you as far as
the ford, to set you on the way."

And we began to walk forward in silence.

"Are ye sorry to leave Essendean ?" said he, after a while.

"Why, sir," said I, "if I knew where I was going, or what
was likely to become of me, I would tell you candidly."

"Ay ?" said Mr. Campbell. "Very well, Davie. Then it behoves me to tell your fortune ; or so far as I may. When
your mother was gone, and your father began to sicken for
his end, he gave me in charge a certain letter, which he said
was your inheritance. 'So soon,' says he, 'as I am gone, give
my boy this letter into his hand, and start him off to the
house of Shaws, not far from Cramond. That is the place I
came from,' he said, 'and it's where it befits that my boy
should return'."

"The house of Shaws !" I cried. "What had my poor father to do with the house of Shaws ?"

"Nay," said Mr. Campbell, "who can tell that for a surety? But the name of that family, Davie, boy, is the name you bear—Balfours of Shaws: an ancient, honest, reputable house, peradventure in these latter days decayed. Your father, too, was a man of learning as befitted his position; no man more plausibly conducted school. Here is the testamentary letter itself, superscribed by the own hand of our departed brother."

He gave me the letter, which was addressed in these words: "To the hands of Ebenezer Balfour, Esquire, of Shaws, in his house of Shaws, these will be delivered by my son, David Balfour." My heart was beating hard at this great prospect now suddenly opening before a lad of seventeen years of age, the son of a poor country dominie in the Forest of Ettrick.

"Mr. Campbell," I stammered, "and if you were in my shoes, would you go?"

"Of a surety," said the minister, "that would I, and without a pause. A pretty lad like you should get to Cramond (which is near in by Edinburgh) in two days of walk. If the worst came to the worst, and your high relations (as I cannot but suppose them to be somewhere of your blood) should put you to the door, ye can but walk the two days back again and risp at the manse door. But I would rather hope that ye shall be well received, as your poor father forecast for you, and for anything that I ken come to be a great man in time. And here, Davie, laddie," he resumed, "it lies near upon my conscience to improve this parting, and set you on the right guard against the dangers of the world.

"Be soople, Davie, in things immaterial," said he. "Bear ye this in mind, that, though gentle born, ye have had a country rearing. Dinnae shame us, Davie, dinnae shame us! In yon great, muckle house, with all these domestics, upper and under, show yourself as nice, as circumspect, as quick

4

at the conception, and as slow of speech as any. As for the laird — remember he's the laird; I say no more: honour to whom honour. It's a pleasure to obey a laird; or should be, to the young."

"Well, sir," said I, "it may be; and I'll promise you I'll try to make it so."

"Why, very well said," replied Mr. Campbell heartily. "And now to come to the material, or (to make a quibble) to the immaterial. I have here a little packet which contains four things." He tugged it, as he spoke, and with some great difficulty, from the skirt pocket of his coat. "Of these four things, the first is your legal due; the little pickle money for your father's books and plenishing, which I have bought (as I have explained from the first) in the design of re-selling at a profit to the incoming dominie. The other three are gifties that Mrs. Campbell and myself would be blithe of your acceptance. The first, which is round, will likely please ye best at the first off-go; but, O Davie, laddie, it's but a drop of water in the sea; it'll help you but a step, and vanish like the morning. The second, which is flat and square and written upon, will stand by you through life, like a good staff for the road, and a good pillow to your head in sickness. And as for the last, which is cubical, that'll see you, it's my prayful wish, into a better land."

With that he got upon his feet, took off his hat, then held me at arm's length, looking at me with his face all working with sorrow; and then whipped about, and crying good-bye to me, set off backward by the way that we had come at a sort of jogging run.

I sat down on the boulder the good man had just left, and opened the parcel to see the nature of my gifts. That which he called cubical, I had never had much doubt of; sure enough it was a little Bible, to carry in a plaid-neuk. That which he had called round I found to be a shilling piece; and the

5

third, which was to help me so wonderfully, both in health and sickness all the days of my life, was a little piece of coarse yellow paper, written upon thus in red ink:

"TO MAKE LILLY OF THE VALLEY WATER. — Take the flowers of lilly of the valley and distil them in sack, and drink a spooneful or two as there is occasion. It restores speech to those that have the dumb palsey. It is good against the Gout; it comforts the heart and strengthens the memory; and the flowers, put into a Glasse, close stopt, and set into one hill of ants for a month, then take it out, and you will find a liquor which comes from the flowers, which keep in a vial; it is good, ill or well, and whether man or woman."

And then in the minister's own hand, was added:

"Likewise for sprains, rub it in; and for the cholic, a great spooneful in the hour."

To be sure, I laughed over this; but it was rather tremulous laughter; and I was glad to get my bundle on my staff's end and set out over the ford and up the hill upon the farther side; till, just as I came on the green drove-road running wide through the heather, I took my last look at Kirk Essendean, the trees about the manse, and the big rowans in the kirkyard where my father and my mother lay.

CHAPTER II

I COME TO MY JOURNEY'S END

On the forenoon of the second day, coming to the top of a hill, I saw all the country fall away before me down to the sea; and in the midst of this descent, on a long ridge, the city of Edinburgh smoking like a kiln.

Presently after, I came by a house where a shepherd lived, and got a rough direction for the neighbourhood of Cramond;

and so, from one to another worked my way to the westward of the capital by Colinton, till I came out upon the Glasgow road. And there, to my great pleasure and wonder, I beheld a regiment marching to the fifes, every foot in time; an old red-faced general on a grey horse at the one end, and at the other the company of Grenadiers, with their Pope's hats.

A little farther on, and I was told I was in Cramond Parish, and began to substitute in my inquiries the name of the house of Shaws. It was a word that seemed to surprise those of whom I sought my way. At first I thought the plainness of my appearance, in my country habit, and that all dusty from the road, consorted ill with the greatness of the place to which I was bound. But after two, or maybe three, had given me the same look and the same answer, I began to take it in my head there was something strange about the Shaws itself.

The better to set this fear at rest, I changed the form of my inquiries; and spying an honest fellow coming along a lane on the shaft of his cart, I asked him if he had ever heard tell of a house they called the house of Shaws.

He stopped his cart and looked at me, like the others.

"Ay," said he. "What for?"

"It's a great house?" I asked.

"Doubtless," says he. "The house is a big, muckle house."

"Ay," said I, "but the folk that are in it?"

"Folk?" cried he. "Are ye daft? There's nae folk there — to call folk."

"What?" say I: "not Mr. Ebenezer?"

"Ou, say," says the man; "there's the laird, to be sure, if it's him you're wanting. What'll like be your business, mannie?"

"I was led to think that I would get a situation," I said looking as modest as I could.

"What?" cries the carter, in so sharp a note that his very horse started; and then, "Well, mannie," he added, "it's nane of my affairs; but ye seem a decent-spoken lad; and if ye'll take a word from me, ye'll keep clear of the Shaws."

The next person I came across was a dapper little man in a beautiful white wig, whom I saw to be a barber on his rounds; and knowing well that barbers were great gossips, I asked him plainly what sort of a man was Mr. Balfour of the Shaws.

"Hoot, hoot, hoot," said the barber, "nae kind of a man, nae kind of a man at all."

I cannot well describe the blow this dealt to my illusions. The more indistinct the accusations were, the less I liked them, for they left the wider field to fancy.

It was drawing on to sundown when I met a stout, dark, sour-looking woman coming trudging down a hill; and she, when I put my usual question turned sharp about, accompanied me back to the summit she had just left, and pointed to a great bulk of building standing very bare upon a green in the bottom of the next valley. My heart sank. "That!" I cried.

The woman's face lit up with a malignant anger. "That is the house of Shaws!" she cried. "Blood built it; blood stopped the building of it; blood shall bring it down. See here!" she cried again — "I spit upon the ground, and crack my thumb at it! Black be its fall! If ye see the laird, tell him what ye hear; tell him this makes the twelve hunner and nineteen time that Jennet Clouston has called down the curse on him, and his house, byre and stable, man, guest, and master, wife, miss, or bairn — black, black be their fall!"

And the woman, whose voice had risen to a kind of eldritch sing-song, turned with a skip, and was gone. I stood where she left me, with my hair on end. In those days folk still believed in witches and trembled at a curse.

I sat me down and stared at the house of Shaws. Country folk went by from the fields an I sat there on the side of the ditch. At last the sun went down, and then, right up against the yellow sky, I saw a scroll of smoke go mounting, not much thicker, as it was, and meant a fire, and warmth, and cookery, and some living inhabitant that must have lit it; and this comforted my heart.

So I set forward by a little faint track in the grass that led in my direction. It was very faint indeed to be the only way to a place of habitation; yet I saw no other. Presently it brought me to stone uprights, with an unroofed lodge beside them, and coats of arms upon the top. A main entrance it was plainly meant to be, but never finished; instead of gates of wrought iron, a pair of hurdles were tied across with a straw rope; and as there were no park walls, nor any sign of avenue, the track I was following passed on the right hand of the pillars, and went wandering on toward the house.

The nearer I got to that, the drearier it appeared. It seemed like the one wing of a house that had never been finished. What should have been the inner end stood open on the upper floors, and showed against the sky with steps and stairs of uncompleted masonry. Many of the windows were unglazed, and bats flew in and out like doves out of a dove-cote.

I came forward cautiously, and giving ear as I came, heard some one rattling with dishes, and a little dry, eager cough that came in fits; but there was no sound of speech, and not a dog barked.

The door, as well as I could see it in the dim light, was a great piece of wood all studded with nails; and I lifted my hand with a faint heart under my jacket, and knocked once. Then I stood and waited. The house had fallen into a dead silence; a whole minute passed away, and nothing stirred but the bats overhead. I knocked again, and hearkened again. By this time my ears had grown so accustomed to the quiet, that I could hear the ticking of the clock inside as it slowly counted out the seconds; but whoever was in that house kept deadly still, and must have held his breath.

I was in two minds whether to run away; but anger got the upper hand, and I began instead to rain kicks and buffets on the door, and to shout out aloud for Mr. Balfour. I was in full career, when I heard the cough right overhead, and, jumping back and looking up, beheld a man's head in a tall nightcap, and the bell mouth of a blunderbuss, at one of the first-storey windows.

"It's loaded," said a voice.

"I have come here with a letter," I said, "to Mr. Ebenezer Balfour of Shaws. Is he here?"

"From whom is it?" asked the man with the blunderbuss.

"That is neither here nor there," said I, for I was growing very wroth.

"Well," was the reply, "ye can put it down upon the door-step, and be off with ye."

"I will do no such thing," I cried. "I will deliver it into Mr. Balfour's hands as it was meant I should. It is a letter of introduction."

"A what?" cried the voice sharply.

I repeated what I had said.

"Who are ye, yourself?" was the next question, after a considerable pause.

"I am not ashamed of my name," said I. "They call me David Balfour."

"Is your father dead?"

I was so much surprised at this, that I could find no voice to answer, but stood staring.

"Ay," the man resumed, "he'll be dead, no doubt; and that'll be what brings ye chapping to my door." Another pause, and then defiantly, "Well, man," he said, "I'll let ye in;" and he disappeared from the window.

10

CHAPTER III

I MAKE ACQUAINTANCE OF MY UNCLE

Presently there came a great rattling of chains and bolts, and the door was cautiously opened and shut to again behind me as soon as I had passed.

"Go into the kitchen and touch naething," said the voice; and while the person of the house set himself to replacing the defences of the door, I groped my way forward and entered the kitchen.

As soon as the last chain was up, the man rejoined me. He was a mean, stooping, narrow-shouldered, clay-faced creature, and his age might have been anything between fifty and seventy. His nightcap was of flannel, and so was the nightgown that he wore, instead of coat and waistcoat, over his ragged shirt. He was long unshaved; but what most distressed and even daunted me, he would neither take his eyes away from me nor look me fairly in the face. What he was, whether by trade or birth, was more than I could fathom; but he seemed most like an old, unprofitable serving-man, who should have been left in charge of that big house upon board wages.

"Are ye sharp-set?" he asked, glancing at about the level of my knee. "Ye can eat that drop parritch?"

I said I feared it was his own supper.

"O," said he, "I can do fine wanting it. I'll take the ale, though." He drank the cup about half out, still keeping an eye upon me as he drank; and then suddenly held out his hand. "Let's see the letter," said he.

I told him the letter was for Mr. Balfour: not for him.

"And who do ye think I am?" says he. "Give me Alexander's letter!"

"You know my father's name?"

"It would be strange if I didnae," he returned, "for he was my born brother; and little as ye seem to like either me or my house, or my good parritch, I'm your born uncle, Davie, my man, and you my born nephew. So give us the letter, and sit down and fill your kyte."

If I had been some years younger, what with shame, weariness, and disappointment, I believe I had burst into tears. As it was, I could find no words, neither black nor white, but handed him the letter, and sat down to the porridge with as little appetite for meat as ever a young man had.

Meanwhile, my uncle, stooping over the fire, turned the letter over and over in his hands.

"Do ye ken what's in it?" he asked suddenly.

"You see for yourself, sir," said I, "that the seal has not been broken."

"Ay," said he, "but what brought you here?"

"To give the letter," said I.

"Hoot-toot!" said Uncle Ebenezer, "dinnae fly up in the snuff at me. We'll agree fine yet. And, Davie, my man, if you're done with that bit parritch, I could just take a sup of it myself.

"Ay," he continued, as soon as he had ousted me from the stool and spoon, "they're fine, halesome food — they're grand food, parritch." He murmured a little grace to himself and fell to. "Your father was very fond of this meal, I mind; he was a hearty, if not a great eater; but as for me, I could never do mair than pyke at food." He took a pull at the small beer, which probably reminded him of hospitable duties, for his next speech ran thus: "If ye're dry, ye'll find water behind the door."

To this I returned no answer, standing stiffly on my two feet and looking down upon my uncle with a mighty angry heart.

"Your father's been long dead?" he asked.

"Three weeks, sir," said I.

"He was a secret man, Alexander — a secret, silent man," he continued. "He never said muckle when he was young. He'll never have spoken muckle of me?"

"I never knew, sir, till you told it me yourself, that he had any brother."

"We'll agree fine yet!" he cried. "I'm just as glad I let you in. And now come awa'to your bed."

To my surprise, he lit no lamp or candle, but set forth into the dark passage, groped his way, breathing deeply, up a flight of steps, and paused before a door, which he unlocked. I was close upon his heels, having stumbled after as best I might; and then he bade me go in, for that was my chamber. I did as he bid, but paused after a few steps, and begged a light to go to bed with.

"Hoot-toot, hoot-toot!" said he. "Lights in a house is a thing I dinnae agree with. I'm unco feared of fires. Good night to ye. Davie, my man." And before I had time to add a further protest, he pulled the door to, and I heard him lock me in from the outside.

I did not know whether to laugh or cry. The room was as cold as a well, and the bed, when I had found my way to it, as damp as a peat-hag; but by good fortune I had caught up my bundle and my plaid, and rolling myself in the latter, I lay down upon the floor under lee of the big bedstead, and fell speedily asleep.

With the first peep of day I opened my eyes, to find myself in a great chamber, hung with stamped leather, furnished with fine embroidered furniture, and lit by three fair windows. Ten years ago, or perhaps twenty, it must have been as pleasant a room to lie down or to awake in, as a man could wish; but damp, dirt, disuse, and the mice and spiders had done their worse since then.

Meanwhile the sun was shining outside; and being very cold in that miserable room, I knocked and shouted till my gaoler came and let me out. He carried me to the back of the house, where was a draw-well, and told me to "wash my face there, if I wanted;" and when that was done, I made the best of my own way back to the kitchen, where he had lit the fire and was making the porridge. The table was laid with two bowls and two horn spoons, but the same single measure of small beer. Perhaps my eye rested on this particular with some surprise, and perhaps my uncle observed it; for he spoke up as if in answer to my thought, asking me if I would like to drink ale — for so he called it.

I told him such was my habit, but not to put himself about. "Na, na," said he; "I'll deny you nothing in reason."

He fetched another cup from the shelf; and then to my great surprise, instead of drawing more beer, he poured an accurate half from one cup to the other.

When we had made an end of our meal, my Uncle Ebenezer unlocked a drawer, and drew out of it a clay pipe and a lump of tobacco, from which he cut one fill before he locked it up again. Then he sat down in the sun at one of the windows and silently smoked. From time to time his eyes came coasting round to me, and he shot out one of his questions. Once it was, "And your mother?" and I told him that she, too, was dead.

He seemed to turn this over in his mind; and then, "Davie, my man," said he, "ye've come to the right bit when ye came to your Uncle Ebenezer. I've a great notion of the family, and I mean to do the right by you."

"Uncle Ebenezer," said I, "I've no manner of reason to suppose you mean anything but well by me. For all that, I would have you to know that I have a pride of my own."

He seemed grievously put out. "Hoots-toots," said he, "ca' cannie, man — ca' cannie! Bide a day or two. I'm nae war-

14

lock, to find a fortune for you in the bottom of a parritch bowl; but just you give me a day or two, and say naething to naebody, and as sure as sure, I'll do the right by you."

"Very well," said I, "enough said. If you want to help me, there's no doubt but I'll be glad of it, and none but I'll be grateful."

It seemed to me (too soon, I dare say) that I was getting the upper hand of my uncle; and I began next to say that I must have the bed and bedclothes aired and put to sun-dry.

"Is this my house or yours?" said he, in his keen voice, and then all of a sudden broke off. "Na, na," said he, "I didnae mean that. What's mine is yours, Davie, my man, and what's yours is mine. Blood's thicker than water; and there's naebody but you and me that ought the name." And then on he rambled about the family, and its ancient greatness, and this put it in my head to give him Jennet Clouston's message.

"Dod, David, I'll have her roasted on red peats before I'm by with it! A witch — a proclaimed witch! I'll off and see the session clerk."

And with that he opened a chest, and got out a very old and well-preserved blue coat and waistcoat, and a good enough beaver hat, both without lace. These he threw on anyway, and taking a staff from the cupboard, locked all up again, and was for setting out, when a thought arrested him.

"I cannae leave you by yoursel' in the house," said he. "I'll have to lock you out."

The blood came to my face. "If you lock me out," I said, "it'll be the last you'll see of me in friendship."

He turned very pale, and sucked his mouth in. "This is no the way," he said, looking wickedly at a corner of the floor — "this is no the way to win my favour, David."

"Sir," says I, "with a proper reverence for your age and our common blood, I do not value your favour at a boddle's purchase."

"Well, well," said he, "we must bear and forbear. I'll no go ; that's all that's to be said of it."

"Uncle Ebenezer," I said, "I can make nothing out of this. You use me like a thief ; you hate to have me in this house ; you let me see it, every word and every minute ; it's not possible that you can like me ; and as for me, I've spoken to you as I never thought to speak to any man."

"Na, na ; na, na," he said, very earnestly. "I like you fine ; we'll agree fine yet ; and for the honour of the house I could-nae let you leave the way ye came. Bide here quiet, there's a good lad."

"Well, sir," said I, after I had thought the matter out in silence, "I'll stay a while. It's more just I should be helped by my own blood than strangers; and if we don't agree, I'll do my best it shall be through no fault of mine."

CHAPTER IV

I RUN A GREAT DANGER IN THE HOUSE OF SHAWS

For a day that was begun so ill, the day passed fairly well. In a room next door to the kitchen, where he suffered me to go, I found a great number of books, both Latin and English, in which I took great pleasure all the afternoon.

One thing I discovered, which put me in some doubt. This was an entry on the fly-leaf of a chapbook (one of Patrick Walker's) plainly written by my father's hand and thus conceived : "To my brother Ebenezer on his fifth birthday." Now, what puzzled me was this : That as my father was of course the younger brother, he must either have made some strange error, or he must have written, before he was yet five, an excellent, clear, manly hand of writing...

I tried to get this out of my head ; but though I took down many interesting authors, old and new, history, poetry, and story-book, this notion of my father's hand of writing stuck to me ; and when at lenght I went back into the kitchen, and sat down once more to porridge and small beer, the first thing I said to Uncle Ebenezer was to ask him if my father had not been very quick at his book.

"Alexander ? No him !" was the reply.

This puzzled me yet more ; and a thought coming into my head, I asked if he and my father had been twins.

He jumped upon his stool, and the horn spoon fell out of his hand upon the floor. "What gars ye ask that ?" he said, and he caught me by the breast of the jacket, and looked this time straight into my eyes.

"What do you mean ?" I asked very calmly, for I was far stronger than he, and not easily frightened. "Take your hand from my jacket. This is no way to behave."

My uncle seemed to make a great effort upon himself. "Dod, man, David," he said, "ye shouldnae speak to me about your father. That's where the mistake is." He sat a while and shook, blinking in his plate : "He was all the brother that ever I had."

Now this last passage, this laying of hands upon my person and sudden profession of love for my dead father, went so clean beyond my comprehension that it put me into both fear and hope.

With this notion, all unacknowledged, but nevertheless getting firmly settled in my head, I now began to imitate his convert looks ; so that we sat at table like a cat and a mouse, each stealthily observing the other.

When he had cleared the platter, he got out a single pipeful of tobacco, just as in the morning, turned round a stool into the chimney corner, and sat a while smoking, with his back to me.

"Davie," he said, at length. "I've been thinking;" then he paused, and said it again. "There's a wee bit siller that I half promised ye before ye were born," he continued; "promised it to your father O, naething legal, ye understand; just gentlemen daffing at their wine. Well, I keep it that bit money separate — it was a great expense but a promise is a promise and it has grown by now to be a matter of just precisely — just exactly" — and here he paused and stumbled — "of just exactly forty pounds!" This last he rapped out with a sidelong glance over his shoulder; and the next moment added, almost with a scream, "Scots!"

The pound Scots being the same thing as an English shilling, the difference made by this second thought was considerable; I could see, besides, that the whole story was a lie, invented with some end which it puzzled me to guess; and I made no attempt to conceal the tone of raillery in which I answered.

"O, think again, sir! Pounds sterling, I believe!"

"That's what I said," returned my uncle; "pounds sterling! And if you'll step out-by to the door a minute, just to see what kind of a night it is, I'll get it out to ye and call ye in again."

I did his will, smiling to myself in my contempt that he should think I was so easily to be deceived.

When I was called in again, my uncle counted out into my hand seven and thirty golden guinea pieces; the rest was in his hand, in small gold and silver; but his heart failed him there and he crammed the change into his pocket.

Now, my uncle seemed so miserly that I was struck dumb by this sudden generosity, and could find no words in which to thank him.

Presently he looked towards me sideways.

"And see here," says he, "tit for tat."

I told him I was ready to prove my gratitude in any reasonable degree, and then waited, looking for some monstrous demand. And yet, when at last he plucked up courage to speak, it was only to tell me (very properly, as I thought) that he was growing old and a little broken, and that he would expect me to help him with the house and the bit garden.

I answered and expressed my readiness to serve.

"Well," he said, "let's begin." He pulled out of his pocket a rusty key. "There," says he, "there's the key of the stair-tower at the far end of the house. Ye can only win into it from the outside, for that part of the house is no finished. Gang ye there, and up the stairs, and bring me down the chest that's at the top. There's papers in't," he added.

"Can I have a light, sir?" said I.

"Na," said he, very cunningly. "Nae lights in my house."

"Very well, sir," said I. "Are the stairs good?"

"They're grand," said he; and then as I was going, "Keep to the wall," he added; "there's nae banisters. But the stairs are grand under foot."

Out I went into the night. It had fallen blacker than ever; and I was glad to feel along the wall, till I came the length of the stair-tower door at the far end of the unfinished wing. I had got the key into the keyhole and had just turned it, when all upon a sudden, without sound of wind or thunder, the whole sky lighted up with wildfire and went black again. I had to put my hand over my eyes to get back to the colour of the darkness; and indeed I was already half blinded when I stepped into the tower.

It was so dark inside, it seemed a body could scarce breathe; but I pushed out with foot and hand, and presently struck the wall with the one, and the lowermost round of the stair with the other.

The house of Shaws stood some five full storeys high, not counting lofts. Well, as I advanced, it seemed to me the stair grew airier and a thought more lightsome; and I was wondering what might be the cause of this change, when a second blink of the summer lightning came and went. It was not only that the flash shone in on every side through breaches in the wall, so that I seemed to be clambering aloft upon an open scaffold, but the same passing brightness showed me the steps were of unequal length, and that one of my feet rested that moment within two inches of the wall.

This was the grand stair! I thought; and with the thought, a gust of a kind of angry courage came into my heart. My uncle had sent me here, certainly to run great risks, perhaps to die. I swore I would settle that "perhaps," if I should break my neck for it; got me down upon my hands and knees; and as slowly as a snail, feeling before me every inch, and testing the solidity of every stone, I continued to ascend the stair.

The tower, I should have said, was square; and in every corner the step was made of a great stone of a different shape, to join the flights. Well, I had come close to one of these turns, when feeling forward as usual, my hand slipped upon an edge and found nothing but emptiness beyond it. The stair had been carried no higher: to set a stranger mounting it in the darkness was to send him straight to his death.

But I knew what I wanted now, and turned and groped my way down again, with a wonderful anger in my heart. The door, which I had shut behind me when I left, now stood open, and shed a little glimmer of light; and I thought I could see a figure standing in the rain, quite still, like a man hearkening. And then there came a blinding flash, which showed me my uncle plainly, just where I had fancied him to stand; and hard upon the heels of it, a great towrow of thunder.

Now, whether my uncle thought the crash to be the sound of my fall, or whether he heard in it God's voice denouncing murder, I will leave you to guess. Certain it is, at least, that he was seized on by a kind of panic fear, and that he ran into the house and left the door open behind him. I followed as softly as I could, and, coming unheard into the kitchen, stood and watched him.

He had found time to open the corner cupboard and bring out a great case bottle of acqua vitae, and now sat with his back towards me at the table. Ever and again he would be seized with a fit of deadly shuddering and groan aloud, and carrying the bottle to his lips, drink down the raw spirits by the mouthful.

I stepped forward, came close behind him where he sat, and suddenly clapping my two hands down upon his shoulders — "Ah!" cried I.

My uncle gave a kind of broken cry like a sheep's bleat, flung up his arms and tumbled to the floor like a dead man. I was somewhat shocked at this; but I had myself to look to first of all, and did not hesitate to let him lie as he had fallen. The keys were hanging in the cupboard ; and it was my design to furnish myself with arms before my uncle should come again to his senses and the power of devising evil. In the cupboard were a few bottles, some apparently of medicine; a great many bills and other papers, which I should willingly enough have rummaged, had I had the time; and a few necessaries, that were nothing to my purpose. Thence I turned to the chests. The first was full of meal; the second of moneybags and papers tied into sheaves; in the third, with many other things (and these for the most part clothes), I found a rusty, ugly-looking Highland dirk without the scabbard. This, then, I concealed inside my waistcoat, and turned to my uncle.

"Come, come," said I; "sit up."

"Are ye alive?" he sobbed. "O man, are ye alive?"

"That am I," said I. "Small thanks to you!"

He had begun to seek for his breath with deep sighs. "The blue phial," said he — "in the aumry — the blue phial." His breath came slower still.

I ran to the cupboard, and, sure enough, found there a blue phial of medicine, with the dose written on it on a paper, and that I administered to him with what speed I might.

"It's the trouble," said he, reviving a little; "I have a trouble, Davie. It's the heart."

I set him on a chair and looked at him. It is true I felt some pity for a man that looked so sick, but I was full besides of righteous anger; and I numbered over before him the points on which I wanted explanation; why he lied to me at every word; why he feared that I should leave him, why he disliked it to be hinted that he and my father were twins — "Is that because it is true?" I asked; why he had given me money to which I was convinced I had no claim; and, last of all, why he had tried to kill me. He heard me all through in silence; and then, in a broken voice, begged me to let him go to bed.

"I'll tell ye the morn," he said; "as sure as death I will."

And so weak was he that I could do nothing but consent. I locked him into his room, however, and pocketed the key; and then returning to the kitchen, made up such a blaze as had not shone there for many a long year, and wrapping myself in my plaid, lay down upon the chests and fell asleep.

CHAPTER V

I GO TO THE QUEEN'S FERRY

Much rain fell in the night; and the next morning there blew a bitter wintry wind out of the north-west, driving scattered clouds.

There was now no doubt about my uncle's enmity; there was no doubt I carried my life in my hand, and he would leave no stone unturned that he might compass my destruction.

But I was young and spirited, and like most lads that have been countrybred, I had a great opinion of my shrewdness.

Presently, all swollen with conceit, I went upstairs and gave my prisoner his liberty. He gave me good morning civilly; and I gave the same to him, smiling down upon him from the heights of my sufficiency. Soon we were set to breakfast, as it might have been the day before.

"Well, sir," said I, with a jeering tone, "have you nothing more to say to me?"

He murmured something about a jest, and that he liked a bit of fun; and then, seeing me smile, changed his tone, and assured me he would make all clear as soon as we had breakfasted. I saw by his face that he had no lie ready for me, though he was hard at work preparing one; and I think I was about to tell him so, when we were interrupted by a knocking at the door.

Bidding my uncle sit where he was, I went to open it, and found on the doorstep a half-grown boy in sea-clothes. He had no sooner seen me that he began to dance some steps of the sea-hornpipe (which I had never before heard of, far less seen), snapping his fingers in the air and footing it right cleverly.

"Well," said I, "if you have no business at all I will even be so unmannerly as to shut you out."

"Stay, brother!" he cried. "Have you no fun about you? or do you want to get me thrashed! I've brought a letter from old Heasy-oasy to Mr. Belflower." He showed me a letter as he spoke. "And I say, mate," he added; "I'm mortal hungry."

"Well," said I, "come into the house, and you shall have a bite if I go empty for it."

With that I brought him in and set him down to my own place, where he fell-to greedily on the remains of breakfast, winking to me between whiles, and making many faces, which

I think the poor soul considered manly. Meanwhile, my uncle had read the letter and sat thinking; then, suddenly, he got to his feet with a great air of liveliness, and pulled me apart into the farthest corner of the room.

"Read that," said he, and put the letter in my hand. Here it is, lying before me as I write:

"*The Hawes Inn, at the Queen's Ferry.*

"Sir, — I lie here with my hawser up and down, and send my cabin-boy to informe. If you have any further commands for overseas, to-day will be the last occasion, as the wind will serve us well out of the firth. I will not seek to deny that I have had crosses with your agent Mr. Rankeillor; of which, if not speedily redd up, you may looke to see some losses follow. I have drawn a bill upon you, as per margin, and am, sir, your most obedt., humble servant, ELIAS HOSEASON."

"You see, Davie," resumed my uncle, as soon as he saw that I had done, "I have a venture with this man Hoseason, the captain of a trading brig, the COVENANT, of Dysart. Now, if you and me was to walk over with you lad, I could see the captain at the Hawes, or maybe on board the COVENANT if there was papers to be signed; and so far from a loss of time, we can jog on to the lawyer, Mr. Rankeillor's. He's factor to half the gentry in these parts; and auld man, forby: highly respeckit; and he kenned your father."

I stood awhile and thought. I was going to some place of shipping, which was doubtless populous, and where my uncle durst attempt no violence, and, indeed, even the society of the cabin-boy so far protected me. Once there, I believed I could force on the visit to the lawyer, even if my uncle were now insincere in proposing it; and, perhaps, in the bottom of my heart, I wished a nearer view of the sea and ships. You are to remember I had lived all my life in the inland hills, and just two days before had my first sight of the firth lying like a blue floor and the sailed ships moving on the face of it, no bigger than toys. One thing with another, I made up my mind.

"Very well," says I, "let us go to the Ferry."

The wind, being in that cold quarter the north-west, blew nearly in our faces as we went. It was the month of June; the grass was all white with daisies and the trees with blossom; but, to judge by our blue nails and aching wrists, the time might have been winter and the whiteness a December frost.

Uncle Ebenezer trudged in the ditch, jogging from side to side like an old ploughman coming home from work. He never said a word the whole way; and I was thrown for talk on the cabin-boy. He told me his name was Ransome, and that he had followed the sea since he was nine, but could not say how old he was, as he had lost his reckoning.

I asked him of the brig (which he declared was the finest ship that sailed) and of Captain Hoseason, in whose praises he was equally loud. Heasy-oasy (for so he still named the skipper) was a man, by his account, that minded for nothing either in heaven or earth; one that, as people said, would "crack on all sail into the day of judgment;" rough, fierce, unscrupulous, and brutal; and all this my poor cabin-boy had taught himself to admire as something seamanlike and manly. He would only admit one flaw in his idol. "He ain't no seaman." he admitted. "That's Mr. Shuan that navigates the brig; he's the finest seaman in the trade, only for drink; and I tell you I believe it! Why, look'ere;" and turning down his stocking he showed me a great, raw, red wound that made my blood run cold. "He done that — Mr. Shuan done it," he said, with an air of pride.

"What!" I cried, "do you take such savage usage at his hands? Why, you are no slave, to be so handled!"

25

"No," said the poor moon–calf, changing his tune at once, "and so he'll find. See're;" and he showed me a great case-knife, which he told me was stolen. "O," says he, "let me see him try; I dare him to; I'll do for him! O, he ain't the first!" And he confirmed it with a poor, silly, ugly oath.

I have never felt such pity for any one in this wide world as I felt for that half-witted creature; and it began to come over me that brig COVENANT (for all her pious name) was little better than a hell upon the seas.

"Have you no friends?" said I.

He said he had a father in some English seaport, I forget which "He was a fine man, too," he said; "but he's dead."

"In Heaven's name," cried I, "can you find no reputable life on shore?"

"It's not all as bad as that," says he; "there's worse off than me: there's the twenty-pounders. O laws! you should see them taking on. Why, I've seen a man as old as you, I des-say" — (to him I seemed old) — "ah, and he had a beard, too — well, and as soon as we cleared out of the river, and he had the drug out of his head — my! how he cried and carried on! I made a fine fool of him, I tell you! And then there's little uns, too: oh, little by me! I tell you, I keep them in order. When we carry little uns, I have a rope's end of my own to wallop 'em." And so he ran on, until it came in on me what he meant by twenty-pounders were those unhappy criminals who were sent overseas to slavery in North America, or the still more unhappy innocents who were kidnapped or trepanned (as the word went) for private interest or vengeance.

Just then we came to the top of the hill, and looked down on the Ferry and the Hope. The Firth of Forth (as is very well known) narrows at this point to the width of a good-sized river, which makes a convenient ferry going north, and turns the upper-reach into a land-locked haven for all manner of ships.

We had all three pulled up on the brow of the hill; and now I marched across the road and addressed my uncle. "I think it right to tell you, sir," says I, "there's nothing that will bring me on board that COVENANT."

He seemed to waken from a dream. "Eh?" he said. "What's that?"

I told him over again.

"Well, well," he said, "we'll have to please ye, I suppose. But what are ye standing here for? It's perishing cold; and if I'm no mistaken, they're busking the COVENANT for sea."

CHAPTER VI

WHAT BEFELL AT THE QUEEN'S FERRY

As soon as we came to the inn, Ransome led us up the stair to a small room, with a bed in it, and heated like an oven by a great fire of coal. At a table hard by the chimney, a tall, dark, sober-looking man sat writing. In spite of the heat of the room, he wore a thick sea-jacket, buttoned to the neck, and a tall hairy cap drawn down over his ears; yet I never saw any man, not even a judge upon the bench, look cooler, or more studious and self-possessed, than this ship-captain.

He got to his feet at once, and coming forward, offered his large hand to Ebenezer. "I am proud to see you, Mr. Balfour."

"Captain Hoseason," returned my uncle, "you keep your room unco hot."

"It's a habit I have, Mr. Balfour," said the skipper, "I'm a cold-rife man by my nature; I have a cold blood, sir. There's neither fur, nor flannel — no, sir, nor, hot rum, will warm up what they call the temperature. Sir, it's the same with most men that have been carbonadoed, as they call it, in the tropic seas."

But it chanced that this fancy of the captain's had a great share in my misfortunes. For though I had promised myself not to let my kinsman out of sight, I was both so impatient for a nearer look of the sea, and so sickened by the closeness of the room, that when he told me to "run downstairs and play myself awhile," I was fool enough to take him at his word.

Away I went, therefore, leaving the two men sitting down to a bottle and a great mass of papers; and crossing the road in front of the inn, walked down upon the beach. With the wind in that quarter, only little wavelets, not much bigger that I had seen upon a lake, beat upon the shore. But the weeds were new to me — some green, some brown and long, and some with little bladders that crackled between my fingers.

I looker, too, at the seamen with the skiff — big brown fellows, some in shirts, some with jackets, some with coloured handkerchiefs about their throats, one with a brace of pistols stuck into their pockets, two or three with knotty bludgeons, and all with their case knives. I passed the time of day with on that looked less desperate than his fellows, and asked him of the sailing the brig. He said they would get under way as soon as the ebb set, and expressed his gladness to be out of a port where there were no taverns and fiddlers; but all with such horrifying oaths, that I made haste to get away from him.

This threw me back on Ransome, who seemed the least wicked of that gang, and who soon came out of the inn and ran to me, crying for a bowl of punch. I told him I would give him no such thing, for neither he nor I was of an age for such indulgences. "But a glass of ale you may have, and welcome," said I. He mopped and mowed at me, and called my names; but he was glad to get the ale, for all that; and presently we were set down at a table in the front room of the inn, and both eating and drinking with a good appetite.

Here it occurred to me that, as the landlord was man of that county, I might do well to make a friend of him. I offered him a share, as was much the custom in those days; but he was far too great a man to sit with such poor customers as Ransome and myself, and he was leaving the room, when I called him back to ask if he knew Mr. Rankeillor.

"Hoot, ay," says he, "and a very honest man. And O, by the by," says he, "was it you that came in with Ebenezer?" And when I had told him yes, "Ye'll be no friend of his?" he asked, meaning in the Scottish way, that I would be no relative.

I told him no, none.

"I thought not," said.

I said it seemed that Ebenezer was ill-seen in the country.

"Nae doubt," said the landlord. "He's a wicked auld man. And yet he was ance a fine young fellow, too. But that was before the report gaed abroad about Mr. Alexander; that was like the death of him."

"And what was it?" I asked.

"Ou, just that he had killed him," said the landlord. "Did ye never hear that?"

"And what would he kill him for?" said I.

"And what for, but just to get the place," said he.

"The place?" said I. "The Shaws?"

"Nae other place that I ken," said he.

"Ay, man?" said I. "Is that so? Was my — was Alexander the eldest son?"

"Deed was he," said the landlord. "What else would he have killed him for?"

And with that he went away, as he had been impatient to do from the beginning.

I sat stunned with my good fortune, and could scarce grow to believe that the same poor lad, who had trudged in the dust from Ettrick Forest not two days ago, was now one of the rich of earth, and had a house and broad lands, and might mount his horse to-morrow. All these pleasant things, and a thousand other, crowded into my mind, as I sat staring before me out the inn window, and paying no heed to what I saw ; only I remember that my eye lighted on Captain Hoseason down on the pier among his seamen, and speaking with some authority. And presently he came marching back towards the house, with no mark of a sailor's clumsiness, but carrying his fine, tall figure with a manly bearing, and still with the same sober, grave expression on his face.

The next thing. I heard my uncle calling me, and found the pair in the road together. It was the captain who addressed me, and that with an air (very flattering to a young lad) of grave equality.

"Sir," said he, "Mr. Balfour tells me great things of you; and for my own part, I like your looks. I wish I was for longer here, that we might make the better friends; but we'll make the most of what we have. Ye shall come on board my brig for half an hour, till the ebb sets, and drink a bowl with me."

Now, I longed to see the inside of a ship more than words can tell; but I was not going to put myself in jeopardy, and I told him my uncle and I had an appointment with a lawyer.

"Ay, ay," said he. "He passed me word of that. But ye see, the boat'll set ye ashore at the town pier, and that's but a penny stonecast from Rankeillor's house." And here he suddenly leaned down and whispered in my ear: "Take care of the old fox he means mischief. Come aboard till I can get a word with ye."

In no time we were alongside (where I sat fairly gaping at the ship's height, the strong humming of the tide against its sides, and the pleasant cries of the seamen at their work), Hoseason, declaring that he and I must be the first aboard, ordered a tackle to be sent down from the main-yard. In this I was whipped into the air and set down again on the deck, where the captain stood ready waiting for me, and instantly slipped back his arm under mine.

"But where is my uncle?" said I suddenly.

"Ay," said Hoseason, with a sudden grimness, "That's the point."

I felt I was lost. With all my strength, I plucked myself clear of him and ran to the bulwarks. Sure enough, there was the boat pulling for the town, with my uncle sitting in the stern. I gave a piercing cry — "Help, help! Murder!" — so that both sides of the anchorage rang with it, and my uncle turned round where he was sitting, and showed me a face full of cruelty and terror.

It was the last I saw. Already strong hands had been plucking me back from the ship's side; and now a thunderbolt seemed to strike me; I saw a great flash of fire, and fell senseless.

CHAPTER VII

I GO TO SEA IN THE BRIG *COVENANT* OF DYSART

When I returned again to life, the uproar, the confused and violent movements, shook and deafened me; and presently, to my other pains and distresses, there was added the sickness of an unused landsmann on the sea. In that time of

my adventurous youth, I suffered many hardships; but none
that was so crushing to my mind and body, or lit by so few
hopes, as these first hours aboard the brig.

I had no measure of time; day and night were alike in that
ill-smelling cavern of the ship's bowels where I lay; and the
misery of my situation drew out the hours to double. But
sleep at length stole from me the consciousness of sorrow.

I was wakened by the light of a hand-lantern shining in
my face. A small man of about thirty, with green eyes and
a tangle of fair hair, stood looking down at me.

"Well," said he, "how goes it?"

I answered by a sob; and my visitor then felt my pulse
and temples, and set himself to wash and dress the wound
upon my scalp.

"Ay," said he. "Cheer up! The world's no done; you've
made a bad start of it, but you'll make a better. Have you
had any meat?"

I said I could not look at it: and thereupon he gave me
some brandy and water in a tea pannikin, and left me once
more to myself.

The next time he came to see me, I was lying betwixt
sleep and waking, my eyes wide open in the darkness the sickness quite departed, but succeeded by a horrid giddiness and
swimming that was almost worse to bear.

The glimmer of the lantern, as the trap opened, shone in
like the heaven's sunlight. The man with the green eyes was
the first to descend the ladder, and I noticed that he came
somewhat unsteadily. He was followed by the captain. Neither said a word; but the first set to and examined me, and
dressed my wound as before, while Hoseason looked me in
my face with an odd, black look.

"Now, sir, you see for yourself," said the first: "A high
fever, no appetite, no light, no meat: you see for yourself
what that means."

"I am no conjurer, Mr. Riach," said the captain.

"Give me leave, sir," said Riach; "you've a good head upon your shoulders, and a good Scotch tongue to ask with; but I will leave you no manner of excuse: I want that boy taken out of this hole and put in the forecastle."

"If ye could hold back your hand from the tinpan, Mr. Riach, I would have no complaint to make of ye," returned the skipper; "and, I make bold to say that ye should keep your breath to cool your porridge. We'll be required on deck," he added, in a sharper note, and set one foot upon the ladder.

But Mr. Riach caught him by the sleeve.

"Admitting that you have been paid to do a murder —" he began.

Hoseason turned upon him with a flash.

"What's that?" he cried. "What kind of talk is that?"

"It seems it is the talk that you can understand," said Mr. Riach, looking him steadily in the face.

"Mr. Riach, I have sailed with ye three cruises," replied the captain. "In all that time, sir, ye should have learned to know me: I'm a stiff man, and a dour man; but for what ye say the now —fie, fie! — it comes from a bad heart and a black conscience. If ye say the lad will die —"

"Ay, will he!" said Mr. Riach.

"Well, sir, is not that enough?" said Hoseason. "Flit him where ye please!"

Even in my then state of sickness, I perceived two things; that the mate was touched with liquor, as the captain hinted, and that (drunk or sober) he was like to prove a valuable friend.

Five minutes afterwards my bonds were cut, I was hoisted on a man's back, carried up to the forecastle, and laid in a bunk on some sea-blankets; where the first thing that I did was to lose my senses.

It was a blessed thing indeed to open my eyes again upon the daylight, and to find myself in the society of men. The forecastle was a roomy place enough, set all about with berths, in which the men of the watch below were seated smoking, or lying down asleep. I had no sooner moved, moreover, that one of the men brought me a drink of something healing which Mr. Riach had prepared, and bade me lie still and I should soon be well again.

Here I lay for the space of many days a close prisoner, and not only got my health again, but came to know my companions. They were a rough lot indeed, as sailors mostly are: being men rooted out of all the kindly parts of life, and condemned to toss together on the rough seas, with masters no less cruel.

There was one man, of maybe forty, that would sit on my berthside for hours and tell me of his wife and child. He was a fisher that had lost his boat, and thus been driven to the deep-sea voyaging. Well, it is years ago now: but I have never forgotten him. Indeed, many of these poor fellows (as the event proved) were upon their last cruise; the deep sea and cannibal fish received them; and it is a thankless business to speak ill of the dead.

Among other good deeds that they did, they returned my money, which had been shared among them and though it was about a third short, I was very glad to get it, and hoped great good from it in the land I was going to. The ship was bound for the Carolinas; and you must not suppose that I was going to that place merely as an exile. In those days of my youth, white men were still sold into slavery on the plantations, and that was the destiny to which my wicked uncle had condemned me.

The cabin-boy Ransome (from whom I had first heard of these atrocities) came in at times from the round-house, where he berthed and served, now nursing a bruised limb in silent agony, now raving against the cruelty of Mr. Shuan. It made my heart bleed; but the men had a great respect for the chief mate, who was, as they said, "the only seaman of the whole jing-bang, and none such a bad man when he was sober." Indeed, I found there was a strange peculiarity about our two mates: that Mr. Riach was sullen, unkind, and harsh when he was sober, and Mr. Shuan would not hurt a fly except when he was drinking. I asked about the captain; but I was told drink made no difference upon that man of iron.

I did my best, in the small time allowed me, to make something like a man, or rather I should say something like a boy of the poor creature, Ransome. But his mind was scarce truly human. He could remember nothing of the time before he came to sea; only that his father had made clocks, and had a starling in the parlour, which could whistle. "The North Countrie;" all else had been blotted out in these years of hardship and cruelties.

It was Mr. Riach (Heaven forgive him !) who gave the boy drink; and it was, doubtless, kindly meant; but besides that it was ruin to his health, it was the pitifullest thing in life to see this unhappy, unfriended creature staggering and dancing, and talking he knew not what.

All this time, you should know, the COVENANT was meeting continual head-winds and tumbling up and down against head-seas, so that the scuttle was almost constantly shut, and the forecastle lighted only by a swinging lantern on a beam. I was never allowed to set my foot on deck; you can picture to yourselves how wary of my life I grew to be, and how impatient for a change.

And a change I was to get, as you shall hear; but I must first tell of a conversation I had with Mr. Riach, which puts a little heart in me to bear my troubles. Getting him in a favourable stage of drink (for indeed he never looked near me when he was sober) I pledged him to secrecy, and told him my whole story.

He declared it was like a ballad; that he would do his best to help; that I should have paper, pen, and ink, and write one line to Mr. Campbell and another to Mr. Rankeillor; and that if I had told the truth, ten to one he would be able (with their help) to pull me through and set me in my rights.

"And in the meantime," says he, "keep your heart up. You're not the only one, I'll tell you that. There's many a man hoeing tobacco overseas that should be mounting his horse at his own door at home; many and many !"

CHAPTER VIII

THE ROUND-HOUSE

One night, about eleven o'clock, a man of Mr. Riach's watch (which was on deck) came below for his jacket; and instantly there began to go a whisper about the forecastle that "Shuan had done for him at last." There was no need of a name; we all knew who was meant; but we had scarce time to get the idea rigthly in our heads, far less to speak of it, when the scuttle was again flung open, and Captain Hoseason came down the ladder. He looked sharply round the bunks in the tossing light of the lantern; and then, walking straight up to me, addressed me, to my surprise, in tones of kindness.

"My man," said he, "we want ye to serve in the round-house. You and Ransome are to change berths. Run away aft with ye."

Even as he spoke, two seamen appeared in the scuttle, carrying Ransome in their arms; and the ship at that moment giving a great sheer into the sea, and the lantern swinging, the light fell direct on the boy's face. It was as white as wax, and had a look upon it like a dreadful smile. The blood in me ran cold, and I drew in my breath as if I had been struck.

"Run away aft; run away aft with ye !" cried Hoseason.

And at that I brushed by the sailors and the boy (who neither spoke nor moved), and ran up the ladder on deck.

The round-house, for which I was bound, and where I was now to sleep and serve, stood some six feet above the decks, and considering the size of the brig, was of good dimensions. Inside were a fixed table and bench, and two berths, one for the captain and the other for the two mates, turn and turn about.

A small window with a shutter on each side, and a skylight in the roof, gave it light by day; and after dark there was a lamp always burning. It was burning when I entered, not brigthly, but enought to show Mr. Shuan sitting at the table, with the brandy bottle and a tin pannikin in front of him.

He took no notice of my coming in; nor did he move when the captain followed and leant on the berth beside me, looking darkly at the mate. I stood in great fear of Hoseason, and had my reasons for it; but something told me I need not be afraid of him just then.

Presently Mr. Riach came in. He gave the captain a glance that meant the boy was dead as plain as speaking, and took his place like the rest of us; so that we all three stood without a word, staring down at Mr. Shuan.

All of a sudden he put out his hand to take the bottle; and at that Mr. Riach started forward and caught it away from him, rather by surprise than violence, crying out, with an oath, that there had been too much of this work altogether, and that a judgment would fall upon the ship. And as he spoke (the weahter sliding-doors standing open) he tossed the bottle into the sea.

Mr. Shuan was on his feet in a trice; he still looked dazed, but he meant murder, ay, and would have done it, for the second time that night, had not the captain stepped in between him and his victim.

"Sit down !" roars the captain. "Ye sot and swine, do ye know what ye've done? Ye've murdered the boy !"

Mr. Shuan seemed to understand; for he sat down again, and put up his hand to his brow.

"Well," he said, "he brought me a dirty pannikin !"

At that word .the captain and I and Mr. Riach all looked at each other for a second with a kind of frightened; and then Hoseason walked up to his chief officer, took him by the shoulder, led him across to his bunk, and bade him lie down and go to sleep, as you might speak to a bad child. The murderer cried a little, but he took off his sea-boots and obeyed.

"Ah !" cried Mr. Riach, with a dreadful voice, "ye should have interfered long syne. It's too late now."

"Mr. Riach," said the captain, "this night's work must never be kent in Dysart. The boy went overboard, sir; that's what the story is; and I would give five pounds out of my pocket it was true !" He turned to the table. "What made ye throw the good bottle away?" he added. "There was nae sense in that, sir. Here, David, draw me another. They're in the bottom locker;" and he tossed me a key. "Ye'll need a glass yourself, sir," he added to Riach. "Yon was an ugly thing to see."

That was the first night of my duties; and in the course of the next day I had got well into the run of them. I had to serve at the meals, which the captain took at regular hours, sitting down with the officer who was off duty; all the day through I would be running with a dram to one or other of my three masters; and at night I slept on a blanket thrown on the deck boards at the aftermost end of the round-house, and right in the draught of the two doors. It was a hard and a cold bed; nor was I suffered to sleep without interruption; for some one would be always coming in from deck to get a dram, and when a fresh watch was to be set, two and sometimes all three would sit down and brew a bowl together. How they kept their health, I know not, any more than how I kept my own.

And yet in other ways it was an easy service. There was no cloth to lay; the meals were either of oatmeal porridge or salt junk, except twice a week, when there was duff.

As for Mr. Shuan, the drink, or his crime, or the two together, had certainly troubled his mind. I cannot say I ever saw him in his proper wits. I was pretty sure from the first that he had no clear mind of what he had done.

Altogether it was no very hard life for the time it lasted, which (as you are to hear) was not long. I was fed as the best of them; even their pickles, which were the great dainty, I was allowed my share of; and had I liked I might have been drunk from morning to night, like Mr. Shuan.

The shadow of poor Ransome, to be sure, lay on all four of us, and on me and Mr. Shuan in particular, most heavily. And then I had another trouble of my own. Here I was, doing dirty work for three men that I looked down upon, and one of whom, at least, should have hung upon a gallows; that was for the present; and as for the future, I could only see myself slaving alongside of negroes in the tobacco fields. Mr. Riach, perhaps from caution, would never suffer me to say another word about my story; the captain, whom I tried to approach, rebuffed me like a dog and would not hear a word; and as the days came and went, my heart sank lower and lower, till I was even glad of the work which kept me from thinking.

CHAPTER IX

THE MAN WITH THE BELT OF GOLD

More than a week went by, in which the ill-luck that had hitherto pursued the COVENANT upon this voyage grew yet more strongly marked.

The tenth afternoon there was a falling swell and a thick, wet, white fog that hid one end of the brig from the other. All afternoon, when I went on deck, I saw men and officers listening hard over the bulwarks.

Maybe about ten at night, I was serving Mr. Riach and the captain at their supper, when the ship struck something with a great sound, and we heard voices singing out. My two masters leapt to their feet.

"She's struck !" said Mr. Riach.

"No, sir," said the captain. "We've only run a boat down." And they hurried out.

The captain was in the right of it. We had run down a boat in the fog, and she had parted in the midst and gone to the bottom with all her crew but one. This man had been sitting in the stern as a passenger, while the rest were on the benches rowing. At the moment of the blow, the stern had been thrown into the air, and the man had leapt up and caught hold of the brig's bowsprit. It showed he had luck and much agility and unusual strength, that he should have thus saved himself from such a pass. And yet, when the captain brought him into the round-house, and I set eyes on him for the first time, he looked as cool as I did.

He was smallish in stature, but well set and as nimble as a goat; his face was of a good open expression, but sunburnt very dark, and heavily freckled and pitted with the smallpox; his eyes were unusually light and had a kind of dancing madness in them, that was both engaging and alarming; and when he took off his greatcoat, he laid a pair of fine silver-mounted pistols on the table, and I saw that he was belted with a great sword.

The captain, too, was taking his observations, but rather of the man's clothes than his person. And to be sure, as soon as he had taken off the greatcoat, he showed forth mighty fine for the round-house of a merchant-brig: having a hat with feathers, a red waistcoat, breeches of black plush, and a blue coat with silver buttons and handsome silver lace; costly clothes, though somewhat spoiled with the fog and being slept in.

"I'm vexed, sir, about the boat," says the captain.

"There are some pretty men gone to the bottom," said the stranger, "that I would rather see on the dry land again than half a score of boats."

"Friends of yours?" said Hoseason.

"You have none such friends in your country," was the reply. "They would have died for me like dogs."

"Well, sir," said the captain, still watching him, "there are more men in the world than boats to put them in."

"And that's true, too," cried the other, "and ye seem to be a gentleman of great penetration."

"I have been in France, sir," says the captain, so that it was plain he meant more by the words than showed upon the face of them.

"Why, sir," replied the captain, "I am a true-blue Protestant, and I thank God for it." (It was the first word of any religion I had even heard from him, and I learnt afterwards he was a great churchgoer while on shore.) "But, for all that," says he, "I can be sorry to see another man with his back to the wall."

"Can ye so, indeed?" asked the Jacobite. "Well, sir, to be quite plain with ye, I am one of those honest gentlemen that were in trouble about the years forty-five and six; and (to be quite plain with ye) if I got into the hands of any of the red-coated gentry, it's like it would go hard with me. Now, sir I was for France; and there was a French ship cruising here to pick me up; but she gave us the go-by in the fog — as I wish from the heart that ye had done yoursel' ! And the best that I can say is this: If ye can set me ashore where I was going. I have that upon me will reward you highly for your trouble.

"In France?" says the captain. "No, sir; that I cannot do. But where ye come from — we might talk of that."

And then, unhappily, he observed me standing in my corner, and packed me off to the galley to get supper for the gentleman. I lost no time, I promise you: and when I came back into the round-house, I found the gentleman had taken a money-belt from about his waist, and poured out a guinea or two upon the table. The captain was looking at the guineas, and then at the belt, and then at the gentleman's face; and I thought he seemed excited.

"Half of it," he cried, "and I'm your man !"

The other swept back the guineas into the belt, and put it on again under his waistcoat. "I have told ye, sir," said he. "Thirty guineas on the seaside, or sixty if ye set me on the Linnhe Loch. Take it, if you will; if not, ye can do your worst."

"Ay," said Hoseason. "And if I give ye over to the soldiers ?"

"Ye would make a fool's bargain," said the other. "Now, sir, ye seem to me to be a man that understands things: bring this money within the reach of Government, and how much of it'll come to you?"

"Well," returned the captain, "what must be must be. Sixty guineas, and done. Here's my hand upon it."

"And here's mine," said the other.

And thereupon the captain went out (rather hurriedly, I thought), and left me alone in the round-house with the stranger.

"And so you're a Jacobite?" said I, as I set meat before him.

"Ay," said he, beginning to eat. "And you, by your long face, should be a Whig?"

"Betwixt and between," said I, not to annoy him; for indeed I was as good a Whig as Mr. Campbell could make me.

"And that's naething," said he. "But I'm saying, Mr. Betwixt-and-Between," he added, "this bottle of yours is dry; and it's hard if I'm to pay sixty guineas and be grudged a dram upon the back of it."

"I'll go and ask for the key," said I, and stepped on deck.

The fog was as close as ever, but the swell almost down. The captain and the two officers were in the waist with their heads together. It struck me (I don't know why) that they were after no good; and the first word I heard, when I drew softly near, more than confirmed me.

It was Mr. Riach, crying out as if upon a sudden thought: "Couldn't we wile him out of the round-house?"

"He's better where he is," returned Hoseason; "he hasn't room to use his sword."

"Well, that's true," said Riach; "but he's hard to come at."

"Hut!" said Hoseason. "We can get the man in talk, one upon each side, and pin him by the two arms; or if that'll not hold, sir, we can dake a run by both the doors and get him under hand before he has the time to draw."

At this hearing, I was seized with both fear and anger at these treacherous, greedy, bloody men that I sailed with. My first mind was to run away; my second was bolder.

"Captain," said I, "the gentleman is seeking a dram, and the bottle's out. Will you give me the key?"

They all started and turned about.

"Why, here's our chance to get the firearms!" Riach cried; and then to me: "Hark ye, David," he said, "do ye ken where the pistols are?"

"Ay, ay," put in Hoseason. "David kens; David's a good lad. Ye see, David, my man, yon wild Hielandman is a danger to the ship, besides being a rank foe to ging George, God bless him!"

I had never been so be-Davided since I came on board: but I said Yes, as if all I heard were quite natural.

"The trouble is," resumed the captain, "that all our fire-locks, great and little, are in the round-house under this man's nose; likewise the powder. Now, if I, or one of the officers, was to go in and take them, he would fall to thinking. But a lad like you, David, might snap up a horn and a pistol or two without remark. And if ye can do it cleverly, I'll bear it in mind when it'll be good for you to have friends; and that's when we come to Carolina."

I told him I would do as he wished, though indeed I had scarce breath to speak with. What was I to do? They were dogs and thieves; they had stolen me from my own country; they had killed poor Ransome; and I was to hold the candle to another murder?

I was still arguing it back and forth, and getting no great clearness, when I came into the round-house and saw the Jacobite eating his supper under the lamp; and at that my mind was made up all in a moment.

"Do ye want to be killed?" said I.

He sprang to his feet, and looked a question at me as clear as if he had spoken.

"O!" cried I, "they're all murderers here; it's a ship full of them! They've murdered a boy already. Now it's you."

"Ay, ay," said he; "but they haven't got me yet." And then looking at me curiously, "Will ye stand with me?"

"That will I !" said I. "I am no thief, nor yet murderer. I'll stand by you."

"Why, then," said he. "What's your name?"

"David Balfour," said I; and then, thinking that man with so fine a coat must like fine people, I added for the first time "of Shaws."

"My name is Stewart," he said, drawing himself up. "Alan Breck, they call me."

The round-house was built very strong, to support the breaching of the seas. Of its five apertures, only the skylight and the two doors were large enough for the passage of a man. The doors, besides, could be drawn close; they were of stout oak, and ran in groves, and were fitted with hooks to keep them either shut or open, as the need arose. The one that was already shut I secured in this fashion; but when I was proceeding to slide to the other, Alan stopped me.

"David," said he — "that door, being open, is the best part of my defences."

"It would be yet better shut," says I.

"Not so, David," says he. "Ye see, I have but one face but so long as that door is open and my face to it, the best part of my enemies will be in front of me, where I would aye wish to find them."

Then he gave me from the rack a cutlass (of which there were a few besides the firearms), choosing it with great care, shaking his head and saying he had never in all his life seen poorer weapons; and next he set me down to the table with a powder-horn, a bag of bullets, and all the pistols, which he bade me charge.

Thereupon he stood up in the midst with his face to the door, and drawing his great sword, made trial of the room he had to wield it in.

"I must stick to the point," he said, shaking his head; "and that's a pity, too. It doesn't set my genius, which is all for the upper guard. And now," said he, "do you keep on charging the pistols, and give heed to me."

"First of all," said he, "how many are against us?"

"Fifteen," said I.

Alan whistled. "Well," said he, "that can't be cured. And now follow me. It is my part to keep this door, where I look for the main battle."

"But then, sir," said I, "there is the door behind you, which they may perhaps break in."

"Ay," said he, "and that is a part of your work. No sooner the pistols charged, than ye must climb up into yon bed where ye're handy at the window; and if they lift hand against the door, ye're to shoot. But that's not all. Let's make a bit of a soldier of ye, David. What else have ye to guard?"

"There's the skylight," said I. "But indeed, Mr. Stewart, I would need to have eyes upon both sides to keep the two of them; for when my face is at the one, my back is to the other."

"And that's very true," said Alan. "But have ye no ears to your head?"

"To be sure!" cried I. "I must hear the bursting of the glass!"

"Ye have some rudiments of sens," said Alan grimly.

CHAPTER X

THE SIEGE OF THE ROUND-HOUSE

But now our time of truce was come to an end. Those on deck had waited for my coming till they grew impatient; and scarce had Alan spoken, when the captain showed face in the open door.

"Stand !" cried Alan, and pointed his sword at him.

The captain said nothing to Alan, but he looked over at me with an ugly look. "David," said he. "I'll mind this;" and the sound of his voice went through me with a jar.

Next moment he was gone.

"And now," said Alan, "let your hand keep your head, for the grip is coming."

Alan drew a dirk, which he held in his left hand in case they should run in under his sword. I, on my part, clambered up into the berth with an armful of pistols and something of a heavy heart, and set open the window where I was to watch. It was a small part of the deck that I could overlook, but enough for our purpose.

It came all of a sudden when it did, with a rush of feet and a roar, and then a shout from Alan, and a sound of blows and some one crying out as if hurt. I looked back over my shoulder, and saw Mr. Shuan in the doorway crossing blades with Alan.

"That's him that killed the boy !" I cried.

"Look to your window !" said Alan; and as I turned back to my place, I saw him pass his sword through the mate's body.

It was none too soon for me to look to my own part; for my head was scarce back at the window, before five men, carrying a spare yard for a battering-ram, ran past me and took post to drive the door in. I had never fired with a pistol in my life, and not often with a gun; far less against a fellow-creature. But it was now or never; and just as they swang the yard, I cried out, "Take that !" and shot into their midst.

I must have hit one of them, for he sang out and gave back a step, and the rest stopped as if a little disconcerted. Before they had time to recover, I sent another ball over their heads; and at my third shot (which went as wide as the second) the whole party threw down the yard and ran for it.

Then I looked round again into deck-house. The whole place was full of the smoke of my own firing, just as my ears seemed to be burst with the noise of the shots. But there was Alan, standing as before; only now his sword was running blood to the hilt.

"There's one of your Whigs for ye!" cried Alan; and then turning to me, he asked if I had done much execution.

I told him I had winged one, and thought it was the captain.

"And I've settled two," says he. "No, there is not enough blood let; they'll be back again. To your watch, David. This was but a dram before meat."

I settled back to my place, re-charging the three pistols I had fired, and keeping watch with both eye and ear.

Our enemies were disputing not far off upon the deck. One person spoke most of the time, as though laying down a plan, and first one and then another answered him briefly, like men taking orders. By this, I made sure they were coming on again, and told Alan.

The thought of the sharp swords and the cold steel was strong in me; and presently, when I began to hear stealthy steps and a brushing of men's clothes against the round-house wall, and knew they were taking their places in the dark, I could have found it in my mind to cry out aloud.

All this was upon Alan's side; and I had begun to think my share of the fight was at an end, when I heard some one drop softly on the roof above me.

Then there came a single call on the sea-pipe, and that was the signal. A knot of them made one rush of it, cutlass in hand, against the door; and at the same moment, the glass of the skylight was dashed in a thousand pieces, and a man leaped through and landed on the floor. Before he got his feet, I had clapped a pistol to his back, and might have shot

48

him, too; only at the touch of him (and him alive) my whole flesh misgave me, and I could no more pull the trigger than I could have flown.

He had dropped his cutlass as he jumped, and when he felt the pistol, whipped straight round and laid hold of me, roaring out an oath; and at that either my courage came again, or I grew so much afraid as came to the same thing; for I gave a shriek and shot him in the midst of the body. He gave the most horrible ugly groan and fell to the floor. The foot of a second fellow, whose legs were dangling through the skylight, struck me at the same time upon the head; and at that I snatched another pistol and shot this one through the thigh, so that he slipped through and tumbled in a lump on his companion's body.

Alan, leaping back to get his distance, ran upon the others like a bull, roaring as he went. They broke before him like water turning, and running, and falling one against another in their haste. The sword in his hands flashed like quicksilver into the huddle of our fleeing enemies; and at every flash there came the scream of a man hurt.

The round-house was like a shambles; three were dead inside, another lay in his death agony across the threshold; and there were Alan and I victorious and unhurt.

He came up to me with open arms. "Come to my arms!" he cried, and embraced and kissed me hard upon both cheeks. "David," said he, "I love you like a brother. And O, man," he cried in a kind of ecstasy, "am I no a bonny fighter?"

Thereupon he turned to the four enemies, passed his sword clean through each of them, and tumbeld them out of doors one after the other. As he did so, he kept humming and singing and whistling to himself, like a man trying to recall an air; only what HE was trying was to make one. All the while, the flush was in his face, and his eyes were as bright as a five-yearold child's with a new toy. And presently he sat down upon the table, sword in hand; the air that he was making all the time began to run a little clearer, and then clearer still; and then out he burst with a great voice into a Gaelic song.

> This is the song of the sword of Alan
> The smith made it,
> The fire set it;
> Now it shines in the hand of Alan Breck.
>
> Their eyes were many and bright,
> Swift were they to behold,
> Many the hands they guided;
> The sword was alone.
>
> The dun deer troop over the hill,
> They are many, the hill is one;
> The dun deer vanish,
> The hill remains.
>
> Come to me from the hills of heather,
> Come from the isles of the sea,
> O far-beholding eagles,
> Here is your meat.

In the meanwhile, I was glad to stagger to a seat. There was that tightness on my chest that I could hardly breathe; the thought of the two men I had shot sat upon me like a nightmare; and all upon a sudden, and before I had a guess of what was coming, I began to sob and cry like any child.

Alan clapped my shoulder, and said I was a brave lad and wanted nothing but a sleep.

"I'll take the first watch," said he.

So I made up my bed on the floor; and he took the first spell, pistol in hand and sword on knee, three hours by the captain's watch upon the wall. Then he roused me up, and I took my turn of three hours; before the end of which it was broad day. All my watch there was nothing stirring; and by the banging of the helm, I knew they had even no one at the tiller. Even as it was, I judged by the wailing of a great number of gulls that went crying and fishing round the ship, that she must have drifted pretty near the coast of one of the islands of the Hebrides; and at last, looking out of the door of the round-house, I saw the great stone hills of Skye on the right hand, and, a little more astern, the strange isle of Rum.

CHAPTER XI

THE CAPTAIN KNUCKLES UNDER

Alan and I sat down to breakfast about six of the clock. The floor was covered with broken glass and in a horrid mess of blood, which took away my hunger. In all other ways we were in a situation not agreeable but merry; having ousted the officers from their own cabin, and having to command all the drink in the ship — both wine and spirits — and all the dainty part of what was eatable, such as the pickles and the fine sort of bread. This, of itself, was enough to set us in good humour; but the richest part of it was this, that the two thirstiest men that ever came out of Scotland (Mr. Shuan being dead) were now shut in the fore-part of the ship and condemned to what they hated most — cold water.

"And depend upon it." Alan said, "we shall hear more of them ere long. Ye may keep a man from the fighting but never from his bottle."

We made good company for each other. Alan, indeed, expressed himself most lovingly; and taking a knife from the table, cut me off one of the silver buttons from his coat.

"I had them," says he, "from my father, Duncan Stewart; and now give ye one of them to be a keepsake for last night's work. And wherever ye go and show that button, the friends of Alan Breck will come around you."

As soon as we were through with our meal, he rummaged in the captain's locker till he found a clothesbrush; and then, taking off his coat, began to visit his suit and brush away the stains, with such care and labour as I supposed to have been only usual with women.

He was still so engaged when we were hailed by Mr. Riach from the deck, asking for a parley; and I, climbing through the skylight, and sitting on the edge of it, pistol in hand and with a bold front, though inwardly, in fear of broken glass, hailed him back again and bade him speak out.

"This is a bad job," said he at last, shaking his head.

"It was none of our choosing," said I.

"The captain," says he, "would like to speak with your friend. They might speak at the window."

Thereupon I consulted with Alan, and the parley was agreed to and parole given upon either side; but this was not the whole of Mr. Riach's business, and he now begged me for a dram with such instancy and such reminders of his former kindness, that at last I handed him a pannikin with about a gill of brandy. He drank a part, and then carried the rest down upon the deck, to share it (I suppose) with his superior.

A little after the captain came (as was agreed) to one of the windows, and stood there in the rain, with his arm in a sling, and looking stern and pale, and so old that my heart smote me for having fired upon him.

"Well, well, sir," said the captain, "Ye've made a sore hash of my brig; I haven't hands enough left to work her; and my first officer (whom I could ill spare) has got your sword through-out his vitals, and passed without speech. There is nothing left me, sir, but to put back into the port of Glasgow after hands; and there (by your leave), ye will find them that are better able to talk to you."

"Ay?" said Alan; "and faith, I'll have a talk with them mysel'! Unless there's naebody speaks English in that town, I have a bonny tale for them. Fifteen tarry sailors upon the one side, and a man and halfling boy upon the other! O, man, it's peetiful!"

Hoseason flushed red.

"No," continued Alan, "that'll no do. Ye'll just have to set me ashore as we agreed."

"Ay," said Hoseason, "but my first officer is dead — ye ken best how. There's none of the rest of us acquaint with this coast, sir, and it's one very dangerous to ships."

"I give ye your choice," says Alan. "Set me on dry ground in Appin or Ardgour, or in Morven, or Arisaig, or Morar; or, in brief, where ye please, within thirty miles of my own country; except in a country of the Campbells."

"But all this will cost money, sir," said the captain.

"Well, sir," said Alan, "I am nae weathercock. Thirty guineas, if ye land me on the seaside; and sixty, if ye put me in the Linnhe Loch."

"But see, sir, where we lie, we are but a few hours' sail from Ardnamurchan," said Hoseason. "Give me sixty, and I'll set ye there."

"And I'm to wear my brogues and run jeopardy of the red-coats to please you?" cried Alan. "No, sir; if ye want sixty guineas earn them, and set me in my own country."

"It's to risk the brig, sir," said the captain, "and your own lives along with her."

"Take it or want it," says Alan.

"Could ye pilot us at all?" asked the captain, who was frowning to himself.

"Well, it's doubtful," said Alan. "I'm more of a fighting man (as ye have seen for yoursel') than a sailorman. But I have been often enough picked up and set down upon this coast, and should keen something of the lie of it."

The captain shook his head, still frowning.

"If I had lost less money on this unchancy cruise," says he, "I would see you in a rope's-end before I risked my brig, sir. But be it as ye will."

CHAPTER XII

I HEAR OF THE RED FOX

Before we had done cleaning out the round-house, a breeze sprang up from a little the east of north. This blew off the rain and brought out the sun.

And here I must explain; and the reader would do well to look at a map. On the day when the fog fell and we ran down Alan's boat, we had been running through the little Minch. At dawn after the battle, we lay becalmed to the east of the Isle of Canna or between that and Isle Eriska in the chain of the Long Island. Now to get from there to the Linnhe Loch, the straight course was through the narrows of the Sound of Mull. But the captain had no chart ; he was afraid to trust his brig so deep among the islands; and the wind serving well, he preferred to go by west of Tiree and come up under the southern coast of the great Isle of Mull.

All day the breeze held in the same point, and rather freshened than died down; and towards afternoon, a swell began to set in from round the outer Hebrides. Our course, to go round about the inner isles, was to the west of south, so that at first we had this swell upon our beam, and were much rolled about.

Alan and I sat in the round-house with the doors open on each side and smoked a pipe or two of the captain's fine tobacco. It was at this time we heard each other's stories.

It was I that showed the example, telling him all my misfortune; which he heard with great goodnature. Only, when I came to mention that good friend of mine, Mr. Campbell the minister, Alan fired up and cried out that he hated all that were of that name.

"Why," said I, "he is a man you should be proud to give your hand to."

"I know nothing I would help a Campbell to," says he, "unless it was a leaden bullet."

"Why, Alan," I cried, "what ails ye at the Campbells?"

"Well," says he, "ye ken very well that I am an Appin Stewart, and the Campbells have long harried and wasted those of my name; ay, and got lands of us by treachery — but never with the sword."

"You that are so wasteful of your buttons," said I, "I can hardly think you would be a good judge."

"Ah!" says he, falling again to smiling, "I got my wastefulness from the same man I got the buttons from; and that was my poor father, Duncan Stewart, grace be to him! He was the prettiest man of his kindred; and the best swordsman in the Hielands, David."

"I think he was not the man to leave you rich," said I.

"And that's true," said Alan. "He left me my breeks to cover me, and little besides. And that was how I came to enlist, which was a black spot upon my character at the best of times, and would still be a sore job for me if I fell among the redcoats."

"What," cried I, "were you in the English army?"

"That was I," said Alan. "But I deserted to the right side at Preston Pans — and that's some comfort."

I could scarcely share his view; holding desertion under arms for an unpardonable fault in honour. But for all I was so young, I was wiser than say my thought. "Dear, dear," says I, "punishment is death."

"Ay," said he, "if they got hands on me, it would be a short shrift and a long tow for Alan!"

"And, good heaven, man," cried I, "you that are a condemned rebel, and a deserter, and a man of the French Kings — what tempts ye back into this country? It's a braving of Providence."

"Tut!" says Alan, "I have been back every year since fortysix!"

"And what brings ye, man?" cried I.

"Well, ye see, I weary for my friends and country," said he. "France is a braw place, nae doubt; but I weary for the heather and the deer. And then I have bit things that I attend to. Whiles I pick up a few lads to serve the King of France: recruits, ye see; and that's aye a little money. But the heart of the matter is the business of my chief, Ardshiel."

"I thought they called your chief Appin," said I.

"Ay, but Ardshiel is the captain of the clan," said he, which scarcely cleared my mind. "Ye see, David, he that was all his life so great a man, and come of the blood and bearing the name of kings, is now brought down to live in a French town like a poor and private person. Now, the tenants, of Appin have to pay a rent to King George; but their hearts are staunch, they are true to their chief; and what with love and a bit of pressure, and maybe a threat or two, the poor folk scrape up a second rent for Ardshiel. Well, David, I'm the hand that carried it." And he struck the belt about his body, so that the guineas rang.

"Do they pay both?" cried I.

"Ay, David," said he. "I told a different tale to yon captain man; but this is the truth of it. And it's wonderful to me how little pressure is needed. But that's the handiwork of my good kinsman and my father's friend, James of the Glens; James Stewardt, that is: Ardshiel's half-brother. He it is that gets the money in, and does the management."

This was the first time I heard the name of that James Stewart, who was afterwards so famous at the time of his hanging. But I took little heed at the moment, for all my mind was occupied with the generosity of these poor Highlanders.

"I call it noble," I cried. "I'm a Whig, or little better but I call it noble."

"Ay," said he, "ye're a Whig, but ye're a gentleman; and that's what does it. Now, if ye were one of the cursed race of Campbell, ye would gnash your teeth to hear tell of it. If ye were the Red Fox..." And at that name, his teeth shut together, and he ceased speaking. I have seen many a grim face but never a grimmer than Alan's when he had named the Red Fox.

"And who is the Red Fox?" I asked, daunted, but still curious.

"Who is he?" cried Alan. "Well, and I'll tell you that, when the men of the clans were broken at Culloden, and the good cause went down, and the horses rode over the fetlocks in the best blood of the north, Ardshiel had to flee like a poor deer upon the mountains — he and his lady and his bairns. A fair job we had of it before we got him shipped; and while he still lay in the heather, the English rogues, that couldnae come at his life, were striking at his right. And now, in there steps a man, a Campbell, red-headed Colin of Glenure —"

"Is that him you call the Red Fox?" said I.

"Will ye bring me his brush?" cries Alan fiercely. "Ay, that's the man. In he steps, and gets papers from King George, to be so-called King's factor on the lands of Appin. And at first he sings small, and is hail-fellow-well-met with Sheamus — that's James of the Glens, my chieftain's aent. But by and by, that came to his ears that I have just told you; how the poor commons of Appin, the farmers and the crofters and the boumen, were wringing their very plaids to get a second rent, and sent it overseas for Ardshiel and his poor bairns. What was it ye called it, when I told ye?"

"I called it noble, Alan," said I.

"And you little better than a common Whig!" cries Alan. "But when it came to Colin Roy, the black Campbell blood in him ran wild. He sat gnashing his teeth at the wine table. Well, David, what does he do? He declares all the farms to let. And, thinks he, in his black heart, 'I'll soon get other tenants that'll overbid these Stewarts and Maccols and Macrobs' (for these are all names in my clan, David), 'and then,' thinks he, 'Ardshiel will have to hold his bonnet on a French roadside.'"

"Well," said I, "what followed?"

Alan laid down his pipe, which he had long since suffered to go out, and set his two hands upon his knees.

"Ay," said he, "ye'll never guess that! For these same Stewarts, and Maccolls, and Macrobs (that had two rents to pay, one to King George by stark force, and one to Ardshiel by natural kindness) offered him a better price than any Campbell in all broad Scotland; and far he sent seeking them — as far as to the sides of Clyde and the cross of Edinburgh — seeking, and fleeching, and begging them to come, where there was a Stewart to be starved and a red-headed hound of a Campbell to be pleasured!"

"Well, Alan," said I, "that is a strange story, and a fine one, too. And Whig as I may be, I am glad the man was beaten."

"Him beaten?" echoed Alan. "It's little ye ken of Campbells, and less of the Red Fox. Him beaten? No: nor will be, till his blood's on the hillside! But if the day comes, David, man, that I can find time and leisure for a bit of hunting, there grows not enough leather in all Scotland to hide him from my vengeance!"

"Man, Alan," said I, "ye are neither very wise nor very Christian to blow off so many words of anger. They will do the man ye call the Fox no harm, and yourself no good. Tell me your tale plainly out. What did he next?"

"Well, David." said he, 'since he couldnae be rid of the loyal commons by fair means, he swore he would be rid of them by foul. Ardshiel was to starve: that was the thing he aimed at. And since them that fed him in his exile wouldnae be bought out — right or wrong, he would drive them out. Therefore he sent for lawyers, and papers, and redcoats to stand at his back. And the kindly folk of that country must all pack and tramp, every father's son out of his father's house, and out of the place where he was bred and fed, and played when he was a callant. And who are to succeed them? Bare-leggit beggars!"

"Let me have word," said I. "Be sure if they take less rents, be sure the Government has a finger in the pie. It's not this Campbell's fault, man — it's his orders. And if ye killed this Colin to-morrow, what better would ye be? There would be another factor in his shoes, as fast as spur can drive."

"Ye're a good lad in a fight," said Alan, "but, man! ye have Whig blood in ye !"

And with this Alan fell into a muse, and for a long time sat very sad and silent.

CHAPTER XIII

THE LOSS OF THE BRIG

It was already late at night, and as dark as it ever would be at that season of the year (and that is to say, it was still pretty bright), when Hoseason clapped his head into the round-house door.

"Here," said he, "come out and see if ye can pilot."

"Is this one of your tricks?" asked Alan.

"Do I look like tricks?" cries the Captain. "I have other things to think of — my brig's in danger!"

By the concerned look of his face, and, above all, by the sharp tones in which he spoke of his brig, it was plain to both of us he was in deadly earnest; and so Alan and I, with no great fear of treachery, stepped on deck.

Altogether it was no such ill night to keep the seas in; and I had begun to wonder what it was that sat so heavily upon the captain, when the brig rising suddenly on the top of a high swell, he pointed and cried to us to look. Away on the lee bow, a thing like a fountain rose out of the moonlight sea, and immediately after we heard a low sound of roaring.

"What do ye call that?" asked the captain gloomily.

"The sea breaking on a reef," said Alan. "And now ye ken where it is; and what better would ye have?"

"Ay," said Hoseason, "if it was the only one."

And sure enough, just as he spoke there came a second fountain farther to the south.

"There!" said Hoseason. "Ye see for yourself. If I had kent of these reefs, if I had had a chart, or if Shuan had been spared, it's not sixty guineas, no, nor six hundred, would have made me risk my brig in sic a stoneyard! But you, sir, that was to pilot us, have ye never a word?"

"I'm thinking," said Alan, "these'll be what they call the Torran Rocks."

"Are there many of them?" says the captain.

"Truly, sir, I am nae pilot," said Alan; "but it sticks in my mind there are ten miles of them."

"So?" said Hoseason. "We'll have to haul our wind then, Mr. Riach; we'll have to come as near in about the end of Mull as we can take her, sir; and even then we'll have the land to keep the wind off us, and that stoneyard on our lee. Well, we're in for it now, and may as well crack on."

With that he gave an order to the steersman, and sent Riach to the foretop. There were only five men on deck, counting the officers; these being all that were fit (or, at least, both fit and willing) for their work. So, as I say, it fell to Mr. Riach to go aloft, and he sat there looking out and hailing the deck with news of all he saw.

"The sea to the south is thick," he cried; and then, after a while, "it does seem clearer in by the land."

As we got nearer to the turn of the land the reefs began to be sown here and there on our very path; and Mr. Riach sometimes cried down to us to change the course. Sometimes, indeed, none to soon; for one reef was so close on the brig's weather board that when a sea burst upon it the lighter sprays fell upon her deck and wetted us like rain.

The brightness of the night showed us these perils as clearly as by day, which was, perhaps, the more alarming. It showed me, too, the face of the captain as he stood by the steersman, now on one foot now on the other, and sometimes blowing in his hands, but still listening and looking, and as steady as steel. Neither he nor Mr. Riach had shown well in the fighting; but I saw they were brave in their own trade, and admired them all the more because I found Alan very white.

By this time, now and then sheering to one side or the other to avoid a reef, but still hugging the wind and the land, we had got round Iona and begun to come alongside Mull. The tide at the tail of the land ran very strong, and threw the brig about. Two hands were put to the helm, and Hoseason himself would sometimes lend a help; and it was strange to see three strong men throw their weight upon the tiller, and it (like a living thing) struggle against and drive them back. This would have been the greater danger had not the sea been for some while free of obstacles. Mr. Riach, besides, announced from the top that he saw clear water ahead.

"Ye were right," said Hoseason to Alan. "Ye have saved the brig, sir; I'll mind that when we come to clear accounts."

"Keep her away a point," sings out Mr. Riach. "Reef to windward!"

And just at the same time the tide caught the brig, and threw the wind out of her sails. She came round into the wind like a top, and the next moment struck the reef with such a dunch as threw us all flat upon the deck, and came near to shake Mr. Riach from his place upon the mast.

I think my head must have been partly turned, for I could scarcely understand the things I saw.

Presently I observed Mr. Riach and the seamen busy round the skiff, and still in the same blank, ran over to assist them; and as soon as I set my hand to work, my mind came clear again.

All the time of our working at the boat, I remember only one other thing: that I asked Alan, looking across at the shore, what country it was; and he answered, it was the worst possible for him, for it was the land of the Campbells.

We had one of the wounded men told off to keep a watch upon the sea and cry us warning. Well, we had the boat about ready to be launched, when this man sang out pretty shrill: "For God's sake, hold on!" We knew by his tone, that it was something more than ordinary; and sure enough, there followed a sea so huge that it lifted the brig right up and canted her over on her beam. Whether the cry came too late, or my hold was too weak, I know not; but at the sudden tilting of the ship I was cast clean over the bulwarks into the sea.

I went down, and drank my fill, and then came up, and got a blink of the moon, and then down again. They say a man, sinks the third time for good. I cannot be made like other folk then; for I would not like to write how often I went down, or how often I came up again. All the while, I was being hurled along, and beaten upon and choked, and then swallowed whole; and the thing was so distracting to my wits, that I was neither sorry nor afraid.

Presently, I found I was holding to a spar, which helped me somewhat. And then all of a sudden I was in quiet water, and began to come to myself.

It was the spare yard I had got hold of, and I was amazed to see how far I had travelled from the brig. I hailed her, indeed; but it was plain she was already out of cry.

I now lay quite becalmed, and began to feel that a man can die of cold as well as of drowning. The shores of Earraid were close in; I could see in the moon light the dots of heather and the sparkling of the mica in the rocks.

"Well," thought I to myself, "if I cannot get as far as that, it's strange!"

I had no skill of swimming, Essen Water being small in our neighbourhood; but when I laid hold upon the yard with both arms, and kicked out with both feet, I soon began to find that I was moving. Hard work it was and mortally slow; but in about an hour of kicking and splashing, I had got well in between the points of a sandy bay surrounded by low hills.

The sea was here quite quiet; there was no sound of any surf; the moon shone clear; and I thought in my heart I had never seen a place so desert and desolate. But it was dry land;

and when at last it grew so shallow that I could leave the yard and wade ashore upon my feet, I cannot tell if I was more tired or more grateful. Both at least I was; tired as I never was before that night; and grateful to God as I trust I have been often, though never with more cause.

CHAPTER XIV

THE ISLET

With my stepping ashore I began the most unhappy part of my adventures. It was half-past twelve in the morning, and though the wind was broken by the land, it was a cold night. I dare not sit down (for I thought I should have frozen) but took off my shoes and walked to and fro upon the sand, barefoot, and beating my breast with infinite weariness.

I was afraid to think what had befallen my shipmates. What with my wet clothes and weariness, and my belly that now began to ache with hunger, I had enough to trouble me without that. So I set off eastward along the south coast, hoping to find a house where I might warm myself, and perhaps get news of those I had lost. And at the worst, I considered the sun would soon rise and dry my clothes.

After a little, my way was stopped by a creek or inlet of the sea, which seemed to run pretty deep into the land; and as I had no means to get across, I must needs change my direction to go about the end of it. At first the creek kept narrowing as I had looked to see; but presently to my surprise it began to widen out again. At this I scratched my head, but had still no notion of the truth; until at last I came to a rising ground, and it burst upon me all in a moment that I was cast upon a little barren isle, and cut off on every side by the salt seas.

Instead of the sun rising to dry me, it came on to rain, with a thick mist; so that my case was lamentable.

And now, all at once, the yard came in my head. What had carried me through the roost would surely serve me to cross this creek in safety. With that I set off, undaunted, across the top of the isle, to fetch and carry it back.

I came to the bay at last, more dead than alive; and at the first glance, I thought the yard was something farther out than when I left it. The sand was smooth and firm, and shelved gradually down, so that I could wade out till the water was almost to my neck and the little waves splashed into my face. But at that depth my feet began to leave me, and I durst venture in no further. As for the yard, I saw it bobbing very quietly some twenty feet beyond.

I had borne up well until this last disappointment; but at that I came ashore, and flung myself down upon the sands and wept.

The time I spent upon the island is still so horrible a thought to me, that I must pass it lightly over. I knew indeed that shell-fish were counted good to eat; and among the rocks of the isle I found a great plenty of limpets, which at first I could scarcely strike from their places, not knowing quickness to be needful. There were, besides, some of the little shells that we call buckies; I think periwinkle is the English name. Of these two I made my whole diet, devouring them cold and raw as I found them.

The creek, or strait, that cut off the isle from the mainland of the Ross, opened out on the north into a bay, and the bay again opened into the Sound of Iona; and it was the neighbourhood of this place that I chose to be my home; though if I had thought upon the very name of home in such a spot, I must have burst out weeping.

The shell-fish on which I lived grew there in great plenty; when the tide was out I could gather a peck at a time: and this was doubtless a convenience. But the other reason went deeper. Now, from a little up the hillside over the bay, I could catch a sight of the great, ancient church and the roofs of the people's houses in Iona. And on the other hand, over the low country of the Ross, I saw smoke go up, morning and evening, as if from a homestead in a hollow of the land.

I kept a bright look-out for boats on the Sound or men passing on the Ross. It still rained, and I turned in to sleep, as wet as ever, and with a cruel sore throat, but a little comforted, perhaps, by having said good night to my next neighbours, the people of Iona.

Charles the Second declared a man could stay outdoors more days in a year in the climate of England than in any other. This was very like a king, with a palace at his back and changes of dry clothes. But he must have had better luck on his flight from Worcester than I had on that miserable isle. It was the height of the summer; yet it rained for more than twenty-four hours, and did not clear until the afternoon of the third day.

This was the day of incidents. In the morning I saw a red deer, a buch with a fine spread of antlers, standing in the rain on the top of the island; but he had scarce seen me rise from under my rock, before he trotted off upon the other side. I supposed he must have swum across the strait; though what should bring any creature to Earraid, was more than I could fancy.

A little after, as I was jumping about after my limpets, I was startled by a guinea-piece, which fell upon a rock in front of me and glanced off into the sea. When the sailors gave me my money, again, they kept back not only about a third of the whole sum, but my father's leather purse; so that from that day out, I carried my gold loose in a pocket with a button. I now saw there must be a hole, and clapped my hand to the place in a great hurry. But this was to lock the stable door after the steed was stolen. I had left the shore at Queen's Ferry with near on fifty pounds; now I found no more than two guinea-pieces and a silver shiling.

It is true I picked up a third guinea a little after, where it lay shining on a piece of turf. That made a fortune of three pound and four shillings, English money, for a lad, the rightful heir of an estate, and now starving on an isle at the extreme and of the wild Highlands.

There is a pretty high rock on the north-west of Earraid, which (because it had flat top and overlooked the Sound) I was much in the habit frequenting; not that I ever stayed in one place, save when asleep, my misery giving me no rest. Indeed I wore myself down with continual and aimless goings and comings in the rain.

As soon, however, as the sun came out, I lay down on the top of that rock to dry myself. The comfort of the sunshine is a thing I cannot tell. It set me thinking hopefully of my deliverance, of which I had begun to despair; and I scanned the sea and the Ross with a fresh interest. On the south of my rock, a part of the island jutted out and hid the open ocean, so that a boat could thus come quite near me upon that side, and I be none the wiser.

Well, all of a sudden, a coble with a brown sail and a pair of fishers aboard of it, came flying round that corner of the isle, bound for Iona. I shouted out, and then fell on my knees on the rock and reached up my hands and prayed to them. They were near enough to hear — I could even see the colour of their hair; and there was no doubt that they observed me, for they cried out in the Gaelic tongue, and laughed. But the boat never turned aside, and flew on, right before my eyes, for Iona.

I could not believe such wickedness, and ran along the shore from rock to rock, crying on them piteously; even after they were out of reach of my voice, I still cried and waved to them; and when they were quite gone I thought my heart would have burst.

The next day (which was the fourth of this horrible life of mine) I found my bodily strenght run very low. But the sun shone, the air was sweet, and what I managed to eat of the shell-fish agreed well with me and revived my courage.

I was scarce back on my rock (where I went always the first thing after I had eaten) before I observed a boat coming down the Sound, and with her head, as I thought, in my direction.

I could no longer hold myself back, but ran to the seaside and out, from one rock to another, as far as I could go. It is a marvel I was not drowned; for when I was brought to a stand at last, my legs shook under me, and my mouth was so dry, I must wet it with the sea-water before I was able to shout.

All this time the boat was coming on; and now I was able to perceive it was the same boat and the same two men as yesterday. This I knew by the hair, which the one had of a bright yellow and the other black. But now there was a third man along with them, who looked to be a better class.

As soon as they were come within easy speech, they let down their sail lay quiet. In spite of my supplications, they drew no nearer in, and what frightened me most of all, the new man tee-hee'd with laughter as he talked and looked at me.

Then he stood up in the boat and addressed me a long while, speaking fast and with many wavings of his hand.

I told him I had no Gaelic; and at this he became very angry, and I began to suspect he thought he was talking English. Listening very close, I caught the word "whateffer," several times; but all the rest was Gaelic and might have been Greek and Hebrew for me.

"Whatever," said I, to show him I had caught a word.

"Yes, yes-yes, yes," says he, and then he looked at the other men, as much as to say, "I told you I spoke English," and began again as hard as ever in the Gaelic.

This time I picked out another word, "tide." Then I had a flash of hope. I remembered he was always waving his hand towards the mainland of the Ross.

"Do you mean when the tide is out?" I cried, and could not finish.

"Yes, yes," said he. "Tide."

At that I turned tail upon their boat (where my adviser had once more begun to tee-hee with laughter), leaped back the way I had come, from one stone to another, and set off running across the isle as I had never run before. In about half an hour I came out upon the shores of the creek; and, sure, enough, it was shrunk into a little trickle of water, through which I dashed, not above my knees and landed with a shout on the main island.

A sea-bred boy would not have stayed a day on Earraid; which is only what they call a tidal islet, and except in the bottom of the neaps, can be entered and left twice in every twenty-four hours, either dry-shod, or at the most by wading. Even I, who had the tide going out and in before me in the bay, and even watched for the ebbs, the better to get my shell-fish — even I (I say) if I had sat down to think, instead of raging at my fate, must have soon guessed the secret, and got free.

I have seen wicked men and fools, a great many of both; and believe they both get paid in the end; but the fools first.

CHAPTER XV

THE LAD WITH THE SILVER BUTTON : THROUGH THE ISLE OF MULL

The Ross of Mull, which I had now got upon, was rugged and trackless, like the isle I had just left, being all bog, and briar, and big stone. I aimed as well as I could for the smoke I had seen so often from the island; and with all my great weariness and the difficulty of the way came upon the house in the bottom of a little hollow about five or six at night. It was low and longish, roofed with turf and built of unmortared stones; and on a mound in front of it, an old gentleman sat smoking his pipe in the sun.

With what little English he had, he gave me to understand that my shipmates had got safe ashore, and had broken bread in that very house on the day after.

"Was there one," I asked, "dressed like a gentleman?"

He said they all wore rough greatcoats; but to be sure, the first of them, the one that alone, wore breeches and stockings, while the rest had sailors' trousers.

"Ah," said I, "and he would have a feathered hat?"

He told me no, that he was bareheaded like myself.

At first I thought Alan might have lost his hat; and then the rain came in my mind, and I judged it more likely he had it out of harm's way under his great coat. This set me smiling, partly because my friend was safe, partly to think of his vanity in dress.

And then the old gentleman clapped his hand to his brow, and cried out that I must be the lad with the silver button.

"Why, yes!" said I, in some wonder.

"Well, then," said the old gentleman, "I have a word for you, that you are to follow your friend to his country, by Torosay."

He then asked me how I had fared, and I told him my tale. When I had done, he took me by the hand, led me into his hut (it was no better) and presented me before his wife, as if she had been the Queen and I a duke.

The good woman set oatbread before me and a cold grouse, patting my shoulder and smiling to me all the time, for she had no English; and the old gentleman (not to be behind) brewed me a strong punch out of their country spirit. All the while I was eating, and after that when I was drinking the punch, I would scarce think it believe in my good fortune; and the house, thought it was thick with the peat-smoke and as full of holes as a colander, seemed like a palace.

The punch threw me in a strong sweat and a deep slumber; the good people let me lie; and it was near noon of the next day before I took the road, my throat already easier and my spirits quite restored by good fare and good news. The old gentleman, although I pressed him hard, would take no money, and gave me an old bonnet for my head.

Thought I to myself: "If these are the wild Highlanders, I could wish my own folk wilder."

I not only started late, but I must have wandered nearly half the time. True, I met plenty of people, grubbing in little miserable fields that would not keep a cat, or herding little kine about the bigness of asses. The Highland dress being forbidden by law since the rebellion, and the people condemned to the Lowland habit, which they much disliked, it was strange to see the variety of their array.

To be sure, this was no concern of mine, except in so far as it entertained me by the way. What was much more to the purpose, few had any English, and these few (unless they were of brotherhood of beggars) not very anxious to place it at my service. I knew Torosay to be my destination, and repeated the name to them and pointed; but instead of simply pointing in reply, they would give me a screed of the Gaelic that set me foolish; so it was small wonder if I went out of my road as often as I stayed in it.

At last, about eight at night, and already very weary, I came to a lone house, where I asked admittance, and was refused, until I bethought me of the power of money in so poor a thumb. Thereupon the man of the house, who had hitherto pretended to have no English, and driven me from his door by signals, suddenly began to speak as cleary as was needful, and agreed for five shillings to give me a night's lodging and guide me the next day to Torosay.

Next day we were up before five upon the clock; but my rascal guide got to the bottle at once, and it was three hours before I had him clear of the house, and then (as you shall hear) only for a worse disappointment.

No sooner, however, had we crossed the back of a hill, and got out of sight of the house windows, than he told me Torosay lay right in front, and that a hilltop (which he pointed out) was my best landmark.

"I care very little for that." said I, "since you are going with me."

The impudent cheat answered me in the Gaelic that he had no English.

"My fine fellow," I said, "I know very well your English comes and goes. Tell me what will bring it back? Is it more money you wish?"

"Five shilling mair," said he, "and hersel' will bring ye there."

I reflected a while, and then offered him two, which he accepted greedily, and insisted on having it in his hands at once — "for luck," as he said, but I think it was rather for my misfortune.

The two shillings carried him not quite as many miles; at the end of which distance he sat down upon the wayside and took off his brogues from his feet, like a man about to rest.

I was now red-hot. "Ha!" said I, "have you no more English?"

He said impudently, "No."

At that I boiled over, and lifted my hand to strike him; and he, drawing a knife from his rags, squatted back and grinned at me like a wild cat. At that, forgetting everything but my anger, I ran in upon him, put aside his knife with my left, and struck him in the mouth with the right. I was a strong lad and very angry, and he but a little man; and he went down before me heavily. By good luck, his knife flew out of his hand as he fell.

I picked up both that and his brogues, wished him a good-morning, and set off upon my way, leaving him barefoot and disarmed.

In about half an hour of walk, I overtook a great, ragged man, moving pretty fast but feeling before him with a staff. He was quite blind, and told me he was a catechist, which should have put me at my ease. But his face went against me; it seemed dark and dangerous and secret; and presently, as we began to go on alongside, I saw the steel butt of a pistol sticking from under the flap of his coat-pocket. To carry such a thing meant a fine of fifteen pounds sterling upon the first offence, and transportation to the colonies upon a second. Nor could I quite see why a religious teacher should go armed, or what a blind man could be doing with a pistol.

I told him about my guide, for I was pround of what I had done, and my vanity for once got the heels of my prudence. At the mention of the five shillings he cried out so loud that I made up my mind I should say nothing of the other two, and was glad he could not see my blushes.

"Was it too much?" I asked, a little faltering.

"Too much!" he cries. "Why, I will guide you to Torosay myself for a dram of brandy. And give you the great pleasure of my company (me that is a man of some learning) in the bargain."

I said I did not see how a blind man could be a guide: but at that he laughed aloud, and said his stick was eyes enough for an eagle.

"Ha!" says he, "that's nothing. Would ye believe me now, that before the Act came out, and when there were weapons in this country, I could shoot? Ay, could I!" cries he, and then with a leer, "If ye had such a thing as a pistol here to try with, I would show ye how it's done."

I told him I had nothing of the sort, and gave him a wider berth. If he had known, his pistol stuck at that time quite plainly out of his pocket, and I could see the sun twinkle on the steel of the butt. But by the better luck for me, he knew nothing, thought all was covered, and lied on in the dark.

He then began to question me cunningly, where I came from, whether I was rich, whether I could change a five-shilling piece for him (which he declared he had at that moment in his sporran), and all the time he kept edging up to me and I avoiding him.

Then I told him that, sure enough, I had a pistol in my pocket as well as he, and if he did not strike across the hill due south I would even blow his brains out.

He came at once very polite; and after trying to soften me for some time, but quite in vain, he cursed me once more in Gaelic and took himself off. I watched him striding along, through bog and briar, tapping with his stick, until he turned the end of a hill and disappeared in the next hollow. Then I struck on again for Torosay, much better pleased to be alone than to travel with that man of learning. This was an unlucky day; and these two, of whom I had just rid myself, one after the other, were the two worse men I met with in the Highlands.

At Torosay, on the Sound of Mull and looking over to the mainland of Morven, there was an inn with an innkeeper who was a Maclean, it appeared, of a very high family; for to keep an inn it thought even more genteel in the Highlands than it is with us, perhaps as partaking of hospitality, or perhaps because the trade is idle and drunken. He spoke good English, and finding me to be something of a scholar, tried me in French, where he easily beat me, and then in the Latin in which I don't know which of us did best. This pleasant rivalry put us at once upon friendly terms; and I sat up and drank punch with him (or to be more correct, sat up and watched him drink it), until he was so tipsy that he wept upon my shoulder.

At last, when my landlord could drink no more, he showed me to a bed, and I lay down in very good spirits. Indeed I was by far in better heart and health of body at the end of that long tramp than I had been at the beginning.

CHAPTER XVI

THE LAD WITH THE SILVER BUTTON : ACROSS MORVEN

There is a regular ferry from Torosay to Kinlochaline on the mainland. Both shores of the Sound are in the country of the strong clan of the Macleans, and the people that passed the ferry with me were almost all of that clan. The skipper of the boat, on the other hand, was called Neil Roy Macrob; and since Macrob was one of the names of Alan's clansmen, and Alan himself had sent me to that ferry, I was eager to come to private speech of Neil Roy.

At Kinlochaline I got Neil Roy up on one side on the beach, and said I made sure he was one of Appin's men.

"And what for no?" said he.

"I am seeking somebody," said I; "and it comes in my mind that you will have news of him. Alan Breck Stewart is his name." And very foolishly, instead of showing him the button, I sought to pass a shilling in his hand.

At this he drew back. "I am very much affronted," he said; "and this is not the way that one shentleman should behave to another at all. The man you ask for is in France; but if he was in my sporran," says he, "and your belly full of shillings, I would not hurt a hair upon his body."

I saw I had gone the wrong way to work, and without wasting time upon apologies, showed him the button lying in the hollow of my palm.

"Aweel, aweel," said Neil; "and I think ye might have begun with that end of the stick, whatever! But if ye are the lad with the silver button, all is well, and I have the word to see that ye come safe. But if ye will pardon me to speak plainly," says he, "there is a name that you should never take into your mouth, and that is the name of Alan Breck; and there is a thing that ye would never do, and that is to offer your dirty money to a Hieland shentleman."

It was not very easy to apologize; for I could scarce tell him (what was the truth) that I had never dreamed he would set up to be a gentleman until he told me so. Neil on his part had no wish to prolong his dealings with me, only to fulfil his orders and be done with it; and he made haste to give me my route. This was to lie the night in Kinlochaline in the public inn; to cross Morven the next day to Ardgour, and lie the night in the house of one John of the Claymore, who was warned that I might come; the third day, to be set across one loch at Corran and another at Balachulish, and then ask my way to the house of James of the Glens, at Aucharn in Duror of Appin.

The inn at Kinlochaline was the most beggarly vile place that ever pigs were styed in, full of smoke, vermin, and silent Highlanders. I was not only discontented with my lodgings, but with myself for my mismanagement of Neil, and thought I could hardly be worse off.

Early in my next day's journey I overtook a little, stout, solemn man, walking very slowly with his toes turned out, sometimes reading in a book and sometimes marking the place with his finger, and dressed decently and plainly in something of a clerical style.

This I found to be another catechist, but of a different order from the blind man of Mull: being indeed one of those sent out by the Edinburgh Society for Propagating Christian Knowledge, to evangelize the more savage places of the Highlands. His name was Henderland; he spoke with the broad south-country tongue, which I was beginning to weary for the sound of; and besides common countryship, we soon found we had a more particular bond of interest. For my good friend, the minister of Essendean, had translated into the Gaelic in his by-time a number of hymns and pious books, which Henderland used in his work, and held in great esteem. Indeed, it was one of these he was carrying and reading when we met.

I told him as far in my affairs as I judged wise; as far, that is, as they were none of Alan's; and gave Balachulish as the place I was travelling to, to meet a friend; for I thought Aucharn, or even Duror, would be too particular, and might put him on the scent.

On his part, he told me much of his work and the people he worked among, the hiding priests and Jacobites, the Disarming Act, the dress, and many other curiosities of the time and place. He seemed moderate; blaming Parliament in several points, and especially because they had framed the Act more severely against those who wore the dress than against those who carried weapons.

This moderation put it in my mind to question him of the Red Fox and the Appin tenants; questions which, I thought, would seem natural enough in the mouth of one travelling to that country.

He said it was a bad business. "It's wonderful," said he, "where the tenants find the money, for their life is mere starvation. (Ye don't carry such a thing as snuff, do ye, Mr. Balfour? No. Well, I'm better wanting it.) But these tenants (as I was saying) are doubtless partly driven to it. James Stewart in Duror (that's him they call James of the Glens) it half-brother to Ardshiel, the captain of the clan; and he is a man much looked up to, and drives very hard. And then there's one they call Alan Breck —"

"Ah!" cried I, "what of him?"

"What of the wind that bloweth where it listeth?" said Henderland. "He's here and away; here to-day and gone tomorrow; a fair heather-cat. He might be glowering at the two of us out of yon whin-bush, and I wouldnae wonder! Ye'll no carry such a thing as snuff, will ye?"

I told him no, and that he had asked the same thing more than once.

"It's highly possible," said he, sighing. "But it seems strange ye shouldnae carry it. However, as I was saying, this Alan Breck is a bold, desperate customer, and well kent to be Jame's right hand. His life is forfeit already; he would boggle at naething; and maybe, if a tenant-body was to hang back he would get a dirk in his wame."

"You make a poor story of it all, Mr. Henderland," said I. "If it is all fear upon both sides, I care to hear no more of it."

"Na," said Mr. Henderland, "but there's love too, and selfdenial that should put the like of you and me to shame. There's something fine about it; no perhaps Christian, but humanly fine."

"And what is the King's agent about?" I asked.

"Colin Campbell?" said Henderland. "Putting his head in a bees' byke!"

"He is to turn the tenants out by force, I hear?" said I.

"Yes," said he, "but the business had gone back and forth, as folk say. First, James of the Glens rode to Edinburgh, and got some lawyer (a Stewart, nae doubt — they all hing together like bats in a steeple) and had the proceedings stayed And then Colin Campbell cam' in again, and had the upper hand before the Barons of Exchequer. And now they tell me the first of the tenants are to flit to-morrow. It's to begin at Duror under James's very windows, which doesnae seem wise by my humble way of it."

"Do you think they'll fight?" I asked.

"Well," says Henderland, "they're disarmed — or supposed to be — for there's still a good deal of cold iron lying by in quiet places."

So we continued talking and walking the great part of the day; until at last, Mr. Henderland, after expressing his delight in my company, and satisfaction at meeting with a friend of Mr. Campbell's ("whon," says he, "I will make bold to call that sweet singer of our covenanted Zion"), proposed that I should make a short stage, and lie the night in his house a little beyond Kingairloch. To say truth, I was overjoyed; for I had no great desire for John of the Claymore, and since my double misadventure, first with the guide and next with the gentleman skipper, I stood in some fear of any Highland stranger. Accordingly, we shook hands upon the bargain, and came in the afternoon to a small house, standing alone by the shore of the Linnhe Loch. The sun was already gone from the desert mountains of Ardgour upon the hither side, but shone on those of Appin on the farther; the loch lay as still as a lake, only the gulls were crying round the sides of it; and the whole place seemed solemn and uncouth.

We had no sooner come to the door of Mr. Henderland's dwelling, than to my great surprise (for I was now used to the politeness of Highlanders) he burst rudely past me, dashed into the room, caught up a jar and a small horn spoon, and began ladling snuff into his nose in most excessive quantities. Then he had a hearty fit of sneezing, and looked upon me with a rather silly smile.

"It's vow I took," says he. "I took a vow upon me that I wouldnae carry it. Doubtless it's a great privation; but when I think upon the martyrs, not only to the Scottish Covenant but to other points of Christianity, I think shame to mind it."

Before we went to bed he offered me sixpence to help me on my way, out of a scanty store he kept in the turf wall of his house; at which excess of goodness I knew not what to do. But at last he was so earnest with me, that I thought it the more mannerly part to let him have his way, and so left him poorer than myself.

CHAPTER XVII

THE DEATH OF THE RED FOX

The next day Mr. Henderland found for me a man who had a boat of his own and was to cross the Linnhe Loch that afternoom into Appin, fishing. Him he prevailed on to take me, for he was one of his flock; and in this way I saved a long day's travel and the price of the two public ferries I must otherwise have passed.

At last we came so near the point of land at the entering in of Loch Leven that I begged to be set on shore. My boatman (who was an honest fellow and mindful of his promise to the catechist) would fain have carried me on to Balachulish; but as this was to take me farther from my secret destination, I insisted, and was set ashore at last under the wood of Lettermore (or Lettervore, for I have heard it both ways) in Alan's country of Appin.

Here I was not only troubled by a cloud of stinging midges, but far more by the doubts of my mind. What I ought to do, why I was going to join myself with an outlaw and a would-be murderer like Alan, whether I should not be acting more like a man of sense to tramp back to the south country direct, by my own guidance and at my own charges, and what Mr. Campbell or even Mr. Henderland would think of me if they should ever learn my folly and presumption: these were the doubts that now began to come in on me stronger than ever.

As I was so sitting and thinking, a sound of men and horses came to me through the wood; and presently after, at a turning of the road, I saw four travellers come into view. The way was in this part so rough and narrow that they came single and led their horses by the reins. The first was a great, red-headed gentleman, of an imperious and flushed face, who carried his hat in his hand and fanned himself, for he was in a breathing heat. The second, by his decent black garb and white wig, I correctly took to be a lawyer. The third was a servant, and wore some part of his clothes in tartan, which showed that his master was of a Highland family, and either an outlaw or else in singular good odour with the Government, since the wearing of tartan was against the Act. If I had been better versed in these things, I would have known the tartan to be of the Argyle (or Campbell) colours. This servant had a good-sized portmanteau strapped on his horse, and a net of lemons (to brew punch with) hanging at the saddlebow; as was often enough the custom with luxurious travellers in that part of the country.

As for the fourth, who brought up the tail, I had seen his like before, and knew him at once to be a sheriff's officer.

I had no sooner seen these people coming than I made up my mind (for no reason that I can tell) to go through with my adventure; and when the first came alongside of me, I rose up from the bracken and asked him the way to Aucharn.

"And what seek ye in Aucharn?" said Colin Roy Campbell of Glenure; him they called the Red Fox; for he it was that I had stopped.

"The man that lives there," said I.

He still kept looking at me, as if in doubt.

"Well," said he, at last, "your tongue is bold; but I am no unfriend to plainness. If ye had asked me the way to the door of James Stewart on any other day but this, I would have set ye right and bidden ye God speed. But to-day — eh, Mungo?" And he turned again to look at the lawyer.

But just as he turned there came the shot of a firelock from higher up the hill; and with the very sound of it Glenure fell upon the road.

"O, I am dead!" he cried, several times over.

The lawyer had caught him up and held him in his arms, the servant standing over and clasping his hands. And now the wounded man looked from one to another with scared eyes, and there was change in his voice that went to the heart.

"Take care of yourselves," says he. "I am dead."

He tried to open his clothes as if to look for the wound, but his fingers slipped on the buttons. With that gave a great sigh, his head rolled on his shoulder, and he passed away.

The lawyer said never a word, but his face was as sharp as a pen and as white as the dead man's; the servant broke out into a great noise of crying and weeping, like a child;

and I, on my side, stood staring at them in a kind of horror. The sheriff's officer had run back at the first sound of the shot, to hasten the coming of the soldiers.

I believe it was his movement that brought me to my senses; for he had no sooner done so than I began to scramble up the hill, crying out, "The murderer! the murderer!"

So little a time had elapsed, that when I got to the top of the first steepness, and could see some part of the open mountain, the murderer was still moving away at no great distance. He was a big man, in a black coat, with metal buttons, and carried a long fowling-piece.

At that the murderer gave a little, quick look over his shoulder, and began to run. The next moment he was lost in a fringe of birches; then he came out again on the upper side, where I could see him climbing like a jackanapes, for that part was again very steep; and then he dipped behind a shoulder, and I saw him no more.

I was at the edge of the upper wood, and so now, when I halted and looked back, I saw all the open part of the hill below me.

The lawyer and the sheriff's officer were standing just above the road, crying and waving on me to come back; and on their left, the red-coats, musket in hand, were beginning to struggle singly out of the lower wood.

"Ten pounds if ye take that lad!" cried the lawyer. "He's an accomplice. He was posted here to hold us in talk."

The soldiers began to spread, some of them to run, and others to put up their pieces and cover me; and still I stood.

"Quick, in here among the trees," said a voice, close by. Indeed, I scarce knew what I was doing, but I obeyed; and as I did so, I heard the firelocks band and the balls whistle in the birches.

Just inside the shelter of the trees I found Alan Breck standing, with a fishing-rod. He gave me no salutation;

indeed it was no time for civilities; only "Come !" says he, and set off running along the side of the mountain towards Balachulish; and I, like a sheep, to follow him.

Now we ran among the birches; now stooping behind low humps upon the mountain side; now crawling on all fours among the heather. The pace was deadly: my heart seemed bursting against my ribs; and I had neither time to think nor breath to speak with. Only I remember seeing with wonder that Alan every now and then would straighten himself to his full height and look back; and every time he did so, there came a great faraway cheering and crying of the soldiers.

Quarter of an hour later, Alan stopped, slapped down flat in the heather, and turned to me.

"Now," said he, "it's earnest. Do as I do, for your life."

And at the same speed, but now with infinitely more precaution, we traced back again across the mountain side by the same way that we had come, only perhaps higher; till at last Alan threw himself down in the upper wood of Littermore, where I had found him at the first, and lay, with his face in the bracken, panting like a dig.

My own sides so ached, my head so swam, my tongue so hung out of my mouth with heat and dryness, that I lay beside him like one dead.

CHAPTER XVIII

I TALK WITH ALAN IN THE WOOD OF LETTERMORE

Alan was the first to come round. He rose, went to the border of the wood, peered out a little, and then returned and sat down.

"Well," said he, "yon was a hot burst, David."

I said nothing, nor so much as lifted my face. I had seen murder done, and a great, ruddy, jovial gentleman struck out of life in a moment; the pity of that sight was still sore within me, and yet that was but a part of my concern. Here was murder done upon the man Alan hated; here was Alan skulking in the trees and running from the troops; and whether his was the hand that fired or only the head that ordered, signified but little. By my way of it, my only friend in that wild country was blood-guilty in the first degree; I held him in horror; I could not look upon his face; I would have rather lain alone in the rain on my cold isle, than in the warm wood beside a murderer.

"Are ye still wearied?" he asked again.

"No," said I, still with my face in the bracken; "no, I am not wearied now, and I can speak. I liked you very well Alan, but your ways are not mine, and they're not God's: and the short and the long of it is just that we must part."

"I will handly twine from ye, David, without some kind of reason for the same," said Alan, mighty gravely. "If ye ken anything against my reputation, it's the least thing that ye should do, for old acquaintance' sake, to let me hear the name of it; and if ye have only taken a distaste to my society, it will be proper for me to judge if I'm insulted."

"Alan," said I, "what is the sens of this? Ye ken very well yon Campbell-man lies in his blood upon the road."

"And I," said Alan, taking out his dirk and laying his hands upon it in a certain manner. "I swear upon the Holy Iron I had neither art nor part, act nor thought in it."

"I thank God for that !" cried I, and offered him my hand. He did not appear to see it.

"And here is a great deal of work about a Campbell !" said he. "They are not so scarce, that I ken !"

„At least," said I, "you cannot justly blame me, for you know very well what you told me in the brig. But the temptation and the act are different, I thank God again for that. We may all be tempted; but to take a life in cold blood, Alan!" And I could say no more for the moment. "And do you know who did it?" I added. "Do you know that man in the black coat?"

"I have nae clear mind about his coat," said Alan cunningly; "but it sticks in my head that it was blue."

"Blue or black, did ye know him?" said I.

"I couldnae just conscientiously swear to him," says Alan. "He gaed very close by me, to be sure, but it's a strange thing that I should just have been tying my brogues."

"Can you swear that you don't know him, Alan?" I cried, half angered, half in a mind to laugh at his evasions.

"Not yet," says he; "but I've a grand memory, for forgetting, David."

"And yet there was one thing I saw clearly," said I; "and that was, that you exposed yourself and me to draw the soldiers."

"It's very likely," said Alan; "and so would any gentleman. You and me were innocent of that transaction."

"The better reason, since we were falsely suspected, that we should get clear," I cried. "The innocent should surely come before the guilty."

"Why, David," said he, "the innocent have aye a chance to get assoiled in court; but for the lad that shot the bullet, I think the best place for him will be the heather."

"Alan," said I, "I'll not say it's the good Christianity as I understand it, but it's good enough. And here I offer ye my hand for the second time."

Whereupon he gave me both of his, saying surely I had cast a spell upon him, for he could forgive me anything. Then he grew very grave, and said we had not much time to throw away, but must both flee that country; he, because he was a deserter, and the whole of Appin would now be searched like a chamber, and every one obliged to give a good account of himself; and I, because I was certainly involved in the murder.

"O !" says I, willing to give him a lesson, "I have no fear of the justice of my country."

"As if this was your country !" said he. "Or as if ye would be tried here, in a country of Stewarts !"

"It's all Scotland," said I.

"Man, I whiles wonder at ye," said Alan. "This is a Campbell that's been killed. Well, it'll be tried in Inverarar, the Campbells' head place; with fifteen Campbells in the jury-box, and the biggest Campbell of all (and that's the Duke) sitting cocking on the bench. Justice, David? The same justice, by all the world, as Glenure found a while ago at the roadside."

This frightened me a little, I confess. I asked him whither we should flee; and as he told me "to the Lowlands," I was a little better inclined to go with him; for, indeed, I was growing impatient to get back and have the upper hand of my uncle. Besides, Alan made so sure there would be no question of justice in the matter, that I began to be afraid he might be right.

"I'll chance it, Alan," said I. "I'll go with you."

"But mind you," said Alan, "it's no small thing. Ye maun lie bare and hard, and brook many an empty belly. Your bed shall be the moorcock's, and your life shall be like the hunted deer's, and ye shall sleep with your hand upon your weapons. Ay, man, ye shall taigle many a weary foot or we get clear ! I tell ye this at the start, for it's a life that I ken well. But if ye ask what other chance ye have, I answer: Nane. Either take to the heather with me, or else hang."

"And that's a choice very easily made," said I; and we shook hands upon it.

So we sat and ate and drank, in a place whence we could see the sun going down into a field of great, wild, and houseless mountains, such as I was now condemned to wander in with my companion.

CHAPTER XIX

THE HOUSE OF FEAR

Night fell as we were walking, and the clouds, which had broken up in the afternoon, settled in and thickened, so that it fell, for the season of the year, extremely dark. The way we went was over rough mountain sides; and though Alan pushed on with an assured manner, I could by no means see how he directed himself.

At last, about half-past ten of the clock, we came to the top of a brae, and saw lights below us. It seemed a house door stood open and let out a beam of fire and candle-light; and all round the house and steading five or six persons were moving hurriedly about each carrying a lighted brand.

Hereupon he whistled three times, in a particular manner. It was strange to see how, at the first sound of it, all the moving torches came to a stand, as if the bearers were affrighted; and how, at the third, the bustle began again as before.

Having thus set folks' mind at rest, we came down the brae, and were met at the yard gate (for this place was like a well-doing farm), by a tall, handsome man of more than fifty, who cried out to Alan in the Gaelic.

"James Stewart," said Alan, "I will ask ye to speak in Scotch for here is a young gentleman with me that has nane of the other. This is him," he added, putting his arm through mine, "a young gentleman of the Lowlands, and a laird in his country, too, but I'm thinking it will be the better for his health, if we give his name the go-by."

James of the Glens turned to me for a moment, and greeted me courteously enough; the next he had turned to Alan.

"This has been a dreadful accident," he cried. "It will bring trouble on the country." And he wrung his hands.

"Hoots," said Alan, "ye must take the sour with the sweet, man. Colin Roy is dead, and be thankful for that !"

While this was going on I looked about me at the servants. Some were on ladders, digging in the thatch of the house or the farm buildings, from which they brought out guns, swords, and different weapons of war, others carried them away; and by the sound of mattock blows from somewhere farther down the brae, I suppose they buried them.

It was about this time that a lassie came out of the hause carrying a pack or bundle; and it has often made me smile to think how Alan's instinct awoke at the mere thought of it.

"What's that the lassie has ?" he asked.

"We're just setting the house in order, Alan," said James, in his frightened and somewhat fawning way. "They'll search Appin with candles, and we must have all things straight. We're digging the bit guns and swords into the moss, ye see; and these, I am thinking will be your ain French clothes. We'll be to bury them, I believe."

"Bury my French clothes !" cried Alan. "Troth, no !" And he laid hold upon the packet and retired into the barn to shift himself, recommending me in the meanwhile to his kinsman.

James carried me accordingly into the kitchen, and sat down with me at table, smiling and talking at first in a very hospitable manner. But presently the gloom returned upon him; he sat frowning and biting his fingers; only remembered me from time to time; and then gave me but a word or two, and a poor smile, and back into his private terrors. His wife sat by the fire and wept, with her face in her hands; his eldest son was crouched upon the floor, running over a great mass of papers and now and again setting one alight and burning it to the bitter end.

This was all wretched for a stranger like myself to hear and see; and I was right glad when Alan returned, looking like himself in his fine French clothes, though (to be sure) they were now grown almost too battered and withered to deserve the name of fine. I was taken out in my turn by another of the sons, and given that change of clothing of which I had stood so long in need, and a pair of Highland brogues made of deer-leather, rather strange at first, but after a little practice very easy to the feet.

By the time I came back Alan must have told his story; for it seemed understood that I was to fly with him, and they were all busy upon our equipment. They gave us each a sword and pistols, though I professed my inability to use the former; and with these, and some ammunition, a bag of oatmeal, an iron pan, and a bottle of right French brandy, we were ready for the heather. Money, indeed, was lacking. I had about two guineas left; Alan's belt having been dispatched by another hand, that trusty messenger had no more than seventeen pence to his whole fortune.

"This'll no do," said Alan.

"Ye must find a safe bit somewhere near by," said James, "and get word sent to me. Ye see, ye'll have to get this business prettily off, Alan. This is no time to be stayed for a guinea or two. They're sure to get wind of ye, sure to seek ye, and by my way of it, sure to lay on ye the wyte of this day's accident."

"Well, and that's true, too," said Alan.

"But see here," said James, "I'll have to offer a reward for ye; ay, will I! It's a sore thing to do between such near friends."

"Ay," said Alan, "I see that."

"And ye'll have to be clear of the country, Alan — ay, and clear of Scotland — you and your friend from the Lowlands too. For I'll have to paper your friend from the Lowlands. Ye see that, Alan — say that ye see that!"

I thought Alan flushed a bit. "This is unco hard on me that brought him here, James," said he, throwing his head back. "It's like making me a traitor!"

"Now, Alan, man!" cried James. "Look things in the face! He'll be papered anyway; Mungo Campbell'll be sure to paper him; what matters if I paper him too!" And then, after a little pause on both, sides; "And, Alan, it'll be a jury of Campbells," said he.

"Well, sir," says Alan, turning to me, "what say ye to that? Ye are here under the safeguard of my honour; and it's my part to see nothing done but what shall please you."

"I have but one word to say," said I; "for to all this dispute I am a perfect stranger. But the plain common sense is to set the blame where it belongs, and that is on the man that fired the shot. Paper him, as ye call it, set the hunt on him; and let honest, innocent folk show their faces in safety."

But at this both Alan and James cried out in horror; bidding me hold my tongue, for that was not to be thought of; and asking me what the Camerons would think? (which confirmed me, it must have been a Cameron from Mamore that did the act) and if I did not see that the lad might be caught?

Thereupon we said farewell, and set out again, bending somewhat eastwards, in a fine mild dark night, and over much the same broken country as before.

CHAPTER XX

THE FLIGHT IN THE HEATHER: *THE ROCKS*

Sometimes we walked, sometimes ran; and as it drew on to morning, walked ever the less and ran the more. For all our hurry, day began to come in while we were still far from any shelter. It found us in a prodigious valley, strewn with rocks and where ran a foaming river. Wild mountains stood around it; there grew there neither grass nor trees; and I have sometimes thought since then, that it may have been the valley called Glencoe, where the massacre was in the time of King William.

The first peep of morning, then, showed us this horrible place, and I could see Alan knit his brow.

"This is no fit place for you and me," he said. "This is a place they're bound to watch."

And with that he ran harder than ever down to the waterside, in a part where the river was split in two among three rocks. It went through with a horrid thundering that made my belly quake; and there hung over the lynn a little mist of spray. Alan looked neither to the right nor to the left, but jumped clean upon the middle rock and fell there on his hands and knees to check himself, for that rock was small and he might have pitched over on the far side. I had scarce time to measure the distance or to understand the peril before I had followed him, and he had caught and stoped me.

So there we stood, side by side, upon a small rock slippery with spray, a far broader leap in front of us, and the river dinning upon all sides. When I saw where I was, there came on me a deadly sickness of fear, and I put my hand over my eyes. Alan took me and shook me; I saw he was speaking, but the roaring of the falls and the trouble of my mind prevented me from hearing; only I saw his face was red with anger, and that he stamped upon the rock. The same look showed me the water raging by, and the mist hanging in the air: and with that I covered my eyes again and shuddered.

The next minute Alan had set the brandy bottle to my lips, and forced me to drink about a gill, which sent the blood into my head again. Then, putting his hands to his mouth, and his mouth to my ear, he shouted, "Hang or drown!" and turning his back upon me, leaped over the farther branch of the stream, and landed safe.

I was now alone upon the rock, which gave me the more room; the brandy was singing in my ears; I had this good example fresh before me, and just wit enough to see that if I did not leap at once, I should never leap at all. I bent low on my knees and flung myself forth, with that kind of anger of despair that has sometimes stood me instead of courage. Sure enough, it was but my hands that reached the full length; these slipped, caught again, slipped again; and I was sliddering back into the lynn, when Alan seized me, first by the hair, then by the collar, and with a great strain dragged me into safety.

Never a word he said, but set off running again for his life, and I must stagger to my feet and run after him. I had been weary before, but now I was sick and bruised, and partly drunken with the brandy; I kept stumbling as I ran, I had a stitch that came near to overmaster me; and when at last Alan paused under a great rock that stood there among a number of others, it was none too soon for David Balfour.

A great rock I have said; but by rights it was two rocks leaning together at the top, both some twenty feet high, and at the first sight inaccessible. Even Alan (though you may say he had as good as four hands) failed twice in an attempt to climb them; and it was only at the third trial, and then by standing on my shoulders and leaping up with such force as I thought must have broken my collarbone, that he secured a lodgement. Once there, he let down his leathern girdle; and with the aid of that and a pair of shallow footholds in the rock, I scrambled up besides him.

Then I saw why we had come there; for the two rocks, being both somewhat hollow on the top and sloping one to the other, made a kind of dish or saucer, where as many as three or four men might have lain hidden.

All this while Alan had not said a word, and had run and climbed with such a savage, silent frenzy of hurry, that I knew he was in mortal fear of some miscarriage. Even now we were on the rock he said nothing, nor so much as relaxed the frowning look upon his face; but clapped flat down, and keeping only one eye above the edge of our place of shelter scouted all round the compass. The dawn had come quite clear; we could see the stony sides of the valley, and its bottom, which was bestrewed with rocks, and the river, which went from one side to another, and made white falls; but nowhere the smoke of a house, nor any living creature but some eagles screaming round a cliff.

Then at last Alan smiled.

"Ay," said he, "now we have a chance. And what's mair," says he, "ye may have observed (you that's a man of so much penetration) that Alan Breck Stewart was perhaps walking quicker than his ordinar'."

"You !" I cried, "you were running fit to burst."

"Was I so ?" said he. "Well, then, ye may depend upon it, there was nae time to be lost. And now here is enough said; gang you to your sleep, lad, and I'll watch."

Accordingly, I lay down to sleep; a little peaty earth had drifted in between the top of the two rocks, and some bracken grew there, to be a bed to me; the last thing I heard was still the crying of the eagles.

I dare say it would be nine in the morning when I was roughly awakened, and found Alan's hand pressed upon my mouth.

"Wheesht !" he whispered. "Ye were snoring."

"Well," said I, surprised at his anxious and dark face, "and why not ?"

He peered over the edge of the rock, and signed to me to do the like.

It was now high day, cloudless, and very hot. The valley was as clear as in a picture. About half a mile up the water was a camp of red-coats; a big fire blazed in their midst, at which some were cooking; and near by, on the top of a rock about as high as ours, there stood a sentry, with the sun sparkling on his arms. All the way down along the riverside were posted other sentries; here near together, there widelier scattered; some planted like the first, on places of command, some on the ground level and marching and counter-marching, so as to meet halfway. Higher up the glen, where the ground was more open, the chain of posts was continued by horse-soldiers, whom we could see in the distance riding to and fro. Lower down, the infantry continued; but as the stream was suddenly swelled by the confluence of a considerable burn, they were more widely set, and only watched the fords and stepping-stones.

I took but one look at them, and ducked again into my place. It was strange indeed to see this valley which had lain so solitary in the hour of dawn, bristling with arms and dotted with the redcoats and breeches.

"Ye see," said Alan, "this was what I was afraid of, Davie; that they would watch the burn-side. They began to come in about two hours ago, and man! but ye're a grand hand at the sleeping! We're in a narrow place. If they get up the sides of the hill, they could easy spy us with a glass; but if they'll only keep in the foot of the valley, we'll do yet. The posts are thinner down the water; and, come night, we'll try our hand at getting by them."

"And what are we to do till night?" I asked.

"Lie here," says he.

You are to remember that we lay on the bare top of a rock, like scones upon a girdle; the sun beat upon us cruelly; the rock grew so heated, a man could scarcely endure the touch of it; and the little patch of earth and fern, which kept cooler, was only large enough for one at a time. We took turn about to lie on the naked rock, which was indeed like the position of that saint that was martyred on a gridiron; and it ran in my mind how strange it was, that in the same climate and at only a few days' distance, I should have suffered so cruelly, first from cold upon my island now from heat upon this rock.

All the while we had no water, only raw brandy for a drink, which was worse than nothing; but we kept the bottle as cool as we could, burying it in the earth and got some relief by bathing our breasts and temples.

The tediousness and pain of these hours upon the rock grew only the greater as the day went on; the rock getting still the hotter and the sun fiercer. There were giddiness, and sickness, and sharp pangs like rheumatism to be supported. I minded then, and have often minded since, on the lines in our Scotch psalm:

> "The moon by night thee shall not smite,
> "Nor yet the sun by day,"

and indeed it was only by God's blessing that we were neither of us sun-smitten.

At last, about two, it was beyond men's bearing, and there was now temptation to resist, as well as pain to thole. For the sun being now got a little into the west, there came a patch of shade on the east side of our rock, which was the side sheltered from the soldiers.

"As well one death as another," said Alan, and slipped over the edge and dropped on the ground on the shadowy side.

I followed him at once, and instantly fell all my length, so weak was I and so giddy with that long exposure. Here, then, we lay for an hour or two, aching from head to foot, as weak as water, and lying quite naked to the eye of any soldier, who should have strolled that way. None came, however, all passing by on the other side; so that our rock continued to be our shield even in this new position.

Presently we began again to get a little strength; and as the soldiers were now lying closer along the riverside, Alan proposed that we should try a start. I was by this time afraid of but one thing in the world; and that was to be set back upon the rock; anything else was welcome to me; so we got ourselves at once in marching order, and began to slip from rock to rock one after the other, now crawling flat on our bellies in the shade, now making a run for it, heart in mouth.

By sundown we had made some distance, even by our slow rate of progress, though to be sure the sentry on the rock was still plainly in our view. But now we came on something that put all fears out of season; and that was a deep rushing burn, that tore down, in that part, to join the glen river. At the sight of this we cast ourselves on the ground and plunged head and shoulders in the water.

We lay there (for the banks hid us), drank again and again, bathed our chests, let our wrists trail in the running water till they ached with the chill; and at last, being wonderfully renewed, we got out the meal-bag and made drammach in the iron pan. This, though it is but cold water mingled with oatmeal, yet makes a good enough dish for a hungry man.

As soon as the shadow of the night had fallen, we set forth again, at first with the same caution, but presently with more boldness, standing our full height and stepping out at a good pace of walking. The moon rose at last and found us still on the road; it was in its last quarter, and was long beset with clouds; but after a while shone out and showed me many dark heads of mountains, and was reflected far underneath us on the narrow arm of a sea-loch.

At this sight we both paused; I struck with wonder to find myself so high and walking (as it seemed to me) upon clouds: Alan to make sure of his direction.

Seemingly he was well pleased, and he must certainly have judged us out of ear-shot of all our enemies, for throughout the rest of our night-march he beguiled the way with whistling of many tunes, warlike, merry, plaintive; reel tunes that made the foot go faster; tunes of my own south country that made me fain to be home from my adventures; and all these, on the great, dark, desert mountains, making company upon the way.

CHAPTER XXI

THE FLIGHT IN THE HEATHER :
THE HEUGH OF CORRYNAKIEGH

Early as day comes in the beginning of July, it was still dark when we reached our destination, a cleft in the head of a great mountain, with a water running through the midst, and upon the one hand a shallow cave in a rock.

The name of the cleft was the Heugh of Corrynakiegh; and although from its height and being so near upon the sea it was often beset with clouds, yet it was on the whole a pleasant place, and the five days we lived in it went happily.

We slept in the cave, making our bed of heather bushes which we cut for that purpose, and covering ourselves with Alan's greatcoat. There was a low concealed place in a turning of the glen, where we were so bold as to make fire; so that we could warm ourselves when the clouds set in, and cook hot porridge, and grill the little trouts that we caught with our hands under the stones and overhanging banks of the burn.

In any by-time Alan must teach me to use my sword, for my ignorance had much distressed him. He made it somewhat more of a pain than need have been, for he stormed at me all through the lessons in a very violent manner of scolding, and would push me so close that I made sure he must run me through the body. I was often tempted to turn tail, but held my ground for all that, and got some profit of my lessons; if it was but to stand on guard with an assured countenance, which is often all that is required.

In the meanwhile, you are not to suppose that we neglected our chief business, which was to get away.

"It will be many a long day," Alan said to me on our first morning, "before the red-coats think upon seeking Corrynakiegh; so now we must get word sent to James, and he must find the siller for us."

"And how shall we send that word?" says I. "We are here in a desert place, which yet we dare not leave; and unless ye get the fowls of the air to be your messengers, I see not what we shall be able to do."

"Ay?" said Alan. "Ye're a man of small contrivance, David."

Thereupon he fell in a muse, looking in the embers of the fire; and presently, getting a piece of wood, he fashioned it in a cross, the four ends of which he blackened on the coals. Then he looked at me a little shyly.

"Could ye lend me my button?" says he. "It seems a strange thing to ask a gift again, but I own I am laith to cut another."

I gave him the button; whereupon he strung it on a strip of his greatcoat which he had used to bind the cross; and tying in a little spring of birch and another of fir, he looked upon his work with satisfaction.

"Now," said he, "when it comes dark again, I will steal down into that clachan, and set this that I have been making in the window of a good friend of mine, John Breck Maccoll."

Says I : "And if he finds it, what is he to think?"

"Well," says Alan, "I wish he was a man of more penetration, for my troth I am afraid he will make little enough of it! But this is what I have in my mind. This cross is something in the nature of the crosstarrie, or fiery cross, which is the signal of gathering in our clans; yet he will know well enough the clan is not to rise, for there it is standing in his window, and no word with it. So he will say to himsel', THE CLAN IS NOT TO RISE, BUT THERE IS SOMETHING. Then he will see my button, and that was Duncan Stewart's. And then he will say to himsel', THE SON OF DUNCAN IS IN THE HEATHER, AND HAS NEED OF ME."

"Well," said I, "it may be. But even supposing so, there is a good deal of heather between there and the Forth."

"And that is a very true word," said Alan. "But then John Breck will see the sprig of birch and the sprig of pine; and he will say to himsel' (if he is a man of any penetration at all, which I misdoubt), ALAN WILL BE LYING IN A WOOD WHICH IS BOTH OF PINES AND BIRCHES. Then he will think to himsel', THAT IS NOT SO VERY RIFE HEREABOUT; and then he will come and give us a look up in Corrynakiegh. And if he does not, David, the devil may fly away with him, for what I care; for he will be no worth the salt to his porridge."

"Eh, man," said I, drolling with him a little, "you're very ingenious! But would it not be simpler for you to write him a few words in black and white?"

"And that is an excellent observe, Mr. Balfour of Shaws," says Alan, drolling with me; "and it would certainly be much simpler for me to write to him, but it would be a sore job for John Breck to read it. He would have to go to the school for two-three years, and it's possible we might be weuried waiting on him."

On that night Alan carried down his fiery cross and set it in the bouman's window. He was troubled when he came back; for the dogs had barked and the folk run out from their houses; and he thought he had heard a clatter of arms and seen a red-coat come to one of the doors. On all accounts we lay the next day in the borders of the wood and kept a close look-out, so that if it was John Breck that came we might be ready to guide him, and if it was the redcoats we should have time to get away.

About noon a man was to be spied, struggling up the open side of the mountain in the sun, and looking round him as he came, from under his hand. No sooner had Alan seen him than he whistled; the man turned and came a little towards us: then Alan would give another "peep!" and the man would come still nearer; and so by the sound of whistling, he was guided to the spot where we lay.

He was a ragged, wild, bearded man, about forty, grossly disfigured with the smallpox, and looked both dull and savage. Although his English was very bad and broken, yet Alan (according to his very handsome use, whenever I was

101

by) would suffer him to speak no Gaelic. Perhaps the strange language made him appear more backward than he really was; but I thought he had little goodwill to serve us, and what he had was the child of terror.

Alan would have him carry a message to James; but the bouman would hear of no message. "She was forget it," he said in his screaming voice; and would either have a letter or wash his hands of us.

I thought Alan would be gravelled at that, for we lacked the means of writing in that desert. But he was a man of more resources than I knew; searched the wood until he found the quill of a cushatdove, which he shaped into a pen; made himself a kind of ink with gunpowder from his horn and water from the running stream; and tearing a corner from his French military commission (which he carried in his pocket, like a talisman to keep him from the gallows), he sat down and wrote as follows:

"Dear Kinsman, — Please send the money by the bearer to the place he kens of.

Your affectionate cousin, A.S."

This he entrusted to the bouman, who promised to make what manner of speed he best could, and carried it off with him down the hill.

He was three full days gone, but about five in the evening of the third, we heard a whistling in the wood, which Alan answered; and presently the bouman came up the waterside, looking for us, right and left. He seemed less sulky than before, and indeed he was no doubt well pleased to have got to the end of such a dangerous commission.

He gave us the news of the country: that it was alive with red-coats; that arms were being found, and poor folk brought in trouble daily; and that James and some of his servants were already clapped in prison at Fort William, under strong suspicion of complicity. It seemed it was noised on all sides that Alan Breck had fired the shot; and there was a bill issued both for him and me, with one hundred pounds reward.

That was all as bad as could be; and the little note the bouman had carried us from Mrs. Stewart was of a miserable sadness. In it she besought Alan not to let himself be captured, assuring him, if he fell in the hands of the troops, both he and James were no better than dead men. The money she had sent was all that she could beg or borrow, and she prayed heaven we could be doing with it. Lastly, she said, she enclosed us one of the bills in which we were described.

This we looked upon with great curiosity and not a little fear, partly as a man may look a mirror, partly as he might look into the barrel of an enemy's gun to judge if it be truly aimed. Alan was advertised as "a small, pock-marked, active man of thirtyfive or thereby, dressed in a feathered hat, a French side-coat of blue with silver buttons, and lace a great deal tarnished, a red waistcoat and breeches of black shag;" and I as "a tall strong lad of about eighteen, wearing an old blue coat, very ragged, an old Highland bonnet, a long home-spun waist-coat, blue breeches; his legs bare, low-country shoes, wanting the toes; speaks like a Lowlander, and has no beard."

Alan was well enough pleased to see his finery so fully remembered and set down; only when he came to the word tarnish, he looked upon his lace like one a little mortified. As for myself, I thought I cut a miserable figure in the bill; and yet was well enough pleased too, for since I had changed these rags, the description had ceased to be a danger and become a source of safety.

"Alan," said I, "you should change your clothes."

"Na, troth!" said Alan, "I have nae others. A fine sight I would be, if I went back to France in a bonnet!"

This put a second reflection in my mind: that if I were to separate from Alan and his tell-tale clothes I should be safe against arrest, and might go openly about my business. Nor was this all; for suppose I was arrested when I was alone, there was little against me; but suppose I was taken in company with the reputed murderer, my case would begin to be grave. For generosity's sake I dare not speak my mind upon this head; but I thought of it none the less.

I thought of it all the more, too, when the bouman brought out a green purse with four guineas in gold and the best part of another in small change. True, it was more than I had. But then Alan, with less than five guineas, had to get as far as France; I, with my less than two, not beyond Queen's Ferry; so that, taking things in their proportion, Alan's society was not only a peril to my life, but a burden on my purse.

But there was no thought of the sort in the honest head of my companion. He believed he was serving, helping, and protecting me. And what should I do but hold my peace, and chafe, and take my chance of it ?

"It's little enough," said Alan, putting the purse in his pocket, "but it'll do my business. And now, John Breck, if ye will hand me over my button, this gentleman and me will be for taking the road."

But the bouman, after feeling about in a hairy purse that hung in front of him in the Highland manner (though he wore otherwise the lowland habit, with sea trousers), began to roll his eyes strangely, and at last said, "Her naisel will loss it," meaning he thought he had lost it.

"What!" cried Alan, "you will lose my button, that was my father's before me? Now I will tell you what is in my mind, John Breck, it is in my mind this is the worse day's work that ever ye did since ye were born."

And as Alan spoke, he set his hands on his knees and looked at the bouman with a smiling mouth, and that dancing light in his eyes that meant mischief to his enemies.

Perhaps the bouman was honest enough; perhaps he had meant to cheat and then, finding himself alone with two of us in a desert place, cast back to honesty as being safer; at least, and all at once, he seemed to find that button and handed it to Alan.

"Well, and it is a good thing for the honour of the Maccolls," said Alan, and then to me. "Here is my button back again, and I thank you for parting with it, which is of a piece with all your friendships to me." Then he took the warmest parting of the bouman. "For," says he, "ye have done very well by me, and set your neck at a venture, I will always give you the name of a good man."

Lastly, the bouman took himself off by one way; and Alan and I (getting our chattels together) struck into another to resume our flight.

CHAPTER XXII

THE FLIGHT IN THE HEATHER: *THE MOOR*

Some seven hours' incessant, hard travelling brought us early in the morning to the end of a range of mountains. In front of us there lay a piece of low, broken desert land, which we must now cross. The sun was not long up, and shone straight in our eyes; a little, thin mist went up from the face of the moorland like a smoke; so that (as Alan said) there might have been twenty squadron of dragoons there and we none the wiser.

We sat down, therefore, in a howe of the hillside till the mist should have risen, and made ourselves a dish of drammach, and held council of war.

"David," said Alan, "this is the kittle bit. Shall we lie here till it comes night, or shall we risk it and stave on ahead?"

"Well," said I, "I am tired indeed, but I could walk as far again, if that was all."

"Ay, but it isnae," said Alan, "nor yet the half. This is how we stand: Appin's fair death to us. To the south it's all Campbells, and no to be thought of. To the north: well, there's no muckle to be gained by going north; neither for you, that wants to get to Queen's Ferry, nor yet for me, that wants to get to France. Well, then, we'll can strike east."

"East be it!" says I, quite cheerily; but I was thinking in to myself: "O, man, if you would take one point of the compass and let me take any other, it would be the best for both of us."

"Well, then, east, ye see, we have the muirs," said Alan. "Once there, David, it's mere pitch-and-toss. Out on yon bald, naked, flat place, where can a body turn to? Let the red-coats come over a hill, they can spy you miles away; and the sorrow's in their horses' heels, they would soon ride you down. It's no good place, David; and I'm free to say, it's worse by daylight than by dark."

"Alan," said I, "hear my way of it. Appin's death for us; we have none too much money, nor yet meal; the longer they seek, the nearer they guess where we are; it's all a risk; and I give my word to go ahead until we drop."

Alan was delighted. "There are whiles," said he, "when ye are altogether too canny and Whiggish to be company for a gentleman like me; but there come other whiles when ye show yoursel' a mettle spark; and it's then, David, that I love ye like a brother."

The mist rose and died away, and showed us that country lying as waste as the sea; only the moorfowl and the peewees crying upon it, and far over to the east, a heard of deer, moving like dots. Much of it was red with heather; much of the rest broken up with bogs and hags and peaty pools; some had been burnt black in a heath fire; and in another place there was quite a forest of dead firs, standing like skeletons. A wearier-looking desert man never saw; but at least it was clear of troops, which was our point.

We went down accordingly into the waste, and began to make our toilsome and devious travel towards the eastern verge. There were the tops of mountains all round (you are to remember) from whence we might be spied at any moment; so it behoved us to keep in the hollow parts of the moor, and when these turned aside from our direction to move up in its naked face with infinite care. Sometimes for half an hour together, we must crawl from one heather bush to another, as hunters do when they are hard upon the deer. It was a clear day again, with a blazing sun; the water in the brandy bottle was soon gone; and altogether, if I had guessed what it would be to crawl half the time upon my belly and walk much of the rest stooping nearly to the knees, I should certainly have held back from such a killing enterprise.

Toiling and resting and toiling again, we wore away the morning; and about noon lay down in a thick bush of heather to sleep. Alan took the first watch, and it seemed to me I had scarce closed my eyes before I was shaken up to take the second. We had no clock to go by; and Alan stuck a sprig of heath in the ground to serve instead; so that as soon as the shadow of the bush should fall so far to the east, I might know to rouse him. But I was by this time so weary that I could have slept twelve hours at a stretch; I had the taste of sleep in my throat; my joints slept even when my mind was waking; the hot smell of the heather, and the drone of the wild bees, were like possets to me; and every now and again I would give a jump and find I had been dozing.

The last time I woke I seemed to come back from farther away, and thought the sun had taken a great start in the heavens. I looked at the sprig of heath, and at that I could have cried aloud: for I saw I had betrayed my trust. My head was nearly turned with fear and shame; and at what I saw when I looked out around me on the moor, my heart was like dying in my body. For sure enough, a body of horse-soldiers had come down during my sleep, and were drawing near to us from the south-east, spread out in the shape of a fan and riding their horses to and fro in the deep parts of the heather.

When I waked Alan, he glanced first at the soldiers, then at the mark and the position of the sun, and knitted his brows with a sudden, quick look, both ugly and anxious which was all the reproach I had of him.

"What have we to do now?" I asked.

"We'll have to play at being hares," said he. "Do ye see yon mountain?" pointing to one on the north-eastern sky.

"Ay," said I.

"Well, then," says he, "let us strike for that. Its name is Ben Alder; it is a wild, desert mountain full of hills and hollows, and if we can win to it before the morn, we may do yet."

With that he began to run forward on his hands and knees with an incredible quickness, as though it were his natural way of going. All the time, too, he kept winding in and out in the lower parts of the moorland where we were the best concealed.

The aching and faintness of my body, the labouring of my heart, the soreness of my hands, and the smarting of my throat had soon grown to be so unbearable that I would gladly have given up. Nothing but the fear of Alan lent me enough of a false kind of courage to continue. As for himself (and you are to bear in mind that he was cumbered with a greatcoat) he had first turned crimson, and as time went on the redness began to be mingled with patches of white; his breath cried and whistled as it came; and his voice, when he whispered his observations in my ear during our halts, sounded like nothing human. Yet he seemed in no way dashed in spirits, nor did he at all abate in his activity; so that I was driven to marvel at the man's endurance.

At length, in the first gloaming of the night, we heard a trumpet sound, and looking back from among the heather, saw the troop beginning to collect. A little after, they had built a fire and camped for the night, about the middle of the waste.

At this I begged and besought that we might lie down and sleep.

"There shall be no sleep the night!" said Alan, "From now on, these weary dragoons of yours will keep the crown of the muirland, and none will get out of Appin but winged fowls. We got through in the nick of time, and shall we jeopard what we've gained? Na, na, when the day comes, it shall find you and me in a fast place on Ben Alder."

"Alan," I said, "it's not the want of will: it's the strenght that I want. If I could, I would; but as sure as I'm alive, I cannot."

"Very well, then" said Alan. "I'll carry ye."

I looked to see if he were jesting; but no, the little man was in dead earnest; and the sight of so much resolution shamed me.

"Lead away!" said I. "I'll follow."

He gave me one look as much as to say, "Well done, David!" and off he set again at his top speed.

By what I have read in books, I think few that have held a pen were ever really wearied, or they would write of it more strongly. I had no care of my life, neither past nor future, and I scarce remembered there was such a lad as David Balfour; I did not think of myself, but just of each fresh step which I was sure would be my last, with despair.

Day began to come in, after years, I thought; and by that time we were past the greatest danger, and could walk upon our feet like men, instead of crawling like brutes. But, dear heart have mercy! what a pair we must have made, going double like old grandfathers, stumbling like babes, and as white as dead folk.

Alan must have been as stupid with weariness as myself, and looked as little where we were going, or we should not have wasked into an ambush like blind men.

It fell in this way. We were going down a heathery brake, Alan leading and I following a pace or two behind, like a fiddler and his wife; when upon a sudden the heather gave a rustle, three or four ragged men leapt out, and the next moment we were lying on our backs, each with a dirk at his throat.

I don't think I cared; the pain of this rough handling was quite swallowed up by the pains of which I was already full; and I was too glad to have stopped walking to mind about a dirk. I lay looking up in the face of the man that held me; and I mind his face was black with the sun and his eyes very light, but I was not afraid of him. I heard Alan and another whispering in the Gaelic; and what they said was all one to me.

Then the dirks were put up, our weapons were taken away, and we were set face to face, sitting in the heather.

"They are Cluny's men," said Alan. "We couldnae have fallen better. We've just to bide here with these, which are his out-sentries, till they can get word to the chief of my arrival."

Now Cluny Macpherson, the chief of the clan Vourich, had been one of the leaders of the great rebellion six years before; there was a price on his life; and I had supposed him long ago in France, with the rest of the heads of that desperate party. Even tired as I was, the surprise of what I heard half wakened me.

That was all the rest I had, until the messenger returned; when, as it appeared that Cluny would be glad to receive us, we must get once more upon our feet and set forward.

CHAPTER XXIII

CLUNY'S CAGE

We came at last to the foot of an exceeding steep wood, which scrambled up a scraggy hillside, and was crowned by a naked precipice.

"It's here," said one of the guides, and we struck up hill.

The trees clung upon the slope, alike sailors on the shrouds of a ship; and their trunks were like the rounds of a ladder, by which we mounted.

Quite at the top, and just before the rocky face of the cliff sprang above the foliage, we found that strange house which was known in the country as "Cluny's Cage." The trunks of several trees had been wattled across, the intervals strengthened with stakes, and the ground behind this barricade levelled up with earth to make the floor. A tree, which grew out from the hillside, was the living centre-beam of the roof. The walls were of wattle and covered with moss. The whole house had something of an egg shape; and it half hung, half stood in that steep, hillside thicket, like a wasp's nest in a green hawthorn.

Within, it was large enough to shelter five or six persons with some comfort. A projection of the cliff had been cunningly employed to be the fireplace; and the smoke rising against the face of the rock, and being not dissimilar in colour, readily escaped notice from below.

This was but one of Cluny's hiding-places; he had caves, besides, and underground chambers in several parts of his country; and following the reports of his scouts, he moved from one to another as the soldiers drew near or moved away. By this manner of living, and thanks to the affection of his clan, he had not only stayed all this time in safety, while so many others had fled or been taken and slain; but stayed four or five years longer, and only went to France at last by the express command of his master. There he soon died; and it is strange to reflect that he may have regretted his Cage upon Ben Alder.

When we came to the door he was seated by his rock chimney, watching a gillie about some cookery. He was mighty plainly habited, with a knitted nightcap drawn over his ears, and smoked a foul cutty pipe. For all that he had the manners of a king, and it was quite a sight to see him rise out of his place to welcome us.

"Well, Mr. Stewart, come away', sir!" said he, "and bring in your friend that as yet I dinnae ken the name of."

"And how is yourself, Cluny?" said Alan. "I hope ye do brawly, sir. And I am proud to see ye, and to present to ye my friend the Laird of Shaws, Mr. David Balfour."

Alan never referred to my estate without a touch of a sneer, when we were alone; but with strangers, he rang the words out like a herald.

"Step in by, the both of ye, gentleman," says Cluny. "I'll make ye welcome to my house, which is a queer, rude place for certain, but one where I have entertained a royal personage, Mr. Stewart — ye doubtless ken the personage I have in my eye. We'll take a dram for luck, and as soon as this handless man of mine has the collops ready, we'll dine and take a hand at the cartes as gentleman should. My life is a bit driegh," says he, pouring out the brandy; "I see little company, and sit and twirl my thumbs, and mind upon a great day that is gone by, and weary for another great day that we all hope will be upon the road. And so here's a toast to ye: The Restoration!"

Thereupon we all touched glasses and drank. I am sure I wished no ill to King George; and if he had been there himself in proper person, it's like he would have done as I did. No sooner had I taken out the dram, than I felt hugely better, and could look on and listen, still a little mistily perhaps, but no longer with the same groundless horror and distress of mind.

It was certainly a strange place, and we had a strange host. In his long hiding, Cluny had grown to have all manner of precise habits, like those of an old maid. He had a particular place, where no one else must sit; the Cage was arranged in a particular way which none must disturb; cookery was one of his chief fancies, and even while he was greeting us in, he kept an eye to the collops.

It appears, he sometimes visited or received visits from his wife and one or two of his nearest friends, under the cover of night; but for the more part lived quite alone, and communicated only with his sentinel and the gillies that waited on him in the Cage. The first thing in the morning, one of them, who was a barber, came and shaved him, and gave him the news of the country, of which he was immoderately greedy. There was no end to his questions; he put them as earnestly as a child, and at some of the answers laughed out of all bounds of reason, and would break out again laughing at the mere memory, hours after the barber was gone.

To be sure, there might have been a purpose in his questions; for though he was thus sequestered, and like the other landed gentlemen of Scotland, stripped by the late Act of Parliament of legal powers, he still exercised a patriarchal justice in his clan. Disputes were brought to him in his hidinghole to be decided; and the men of his country, who would have snapped their fingers at the Court of Session, laid aside revenge and paid down money at the bare word of this forfeited and hunted outlaw. When he was angered, which was often enough, he gave his commands and breathed threats of punishment like any king; and his gillies trembled and crouched away from him like children before a hasty father. With each of them, as he entered, he ceremoniously shook hands, both parties touching their bonnets at the same time in a military manner. Altogether, I had a fair chance to see some of the inner workings of a Highland clan; and this was a proscribed fugitive chief; his country conquered; the troops riding upon all sides in quest of him, sometimes within a mile of where he lay; and when the least of the ragged fellows, whom he rated and threatened, could have made a fortune by betraying him.

On that first day, as soon as the collops were ready, Cluny gave them with his own hand a squeeze of a lemon (for he was well supplied with luxuries) and bade us draw in to our meal.

"They," said he, meaning the collops, "are such as I gave his Royal Highness in this very house; bating the lemon juice, for at that time we were glad to get the meat and never fashed for condiments. Indeed, there were mair dragoons, than lemons in my country in the year forty-six."

I do not know if the collops were truly very good, but my heart rose against the sight of them, and I could eat but little. All the while Cluny entertained us with stories of Prince Charlie's stay in the Cage, giving us the very words of the speakers, and rising from his place to show us where they stood. By these, I gathered the Prince was a gracious, spirited boy, like the son of a race of polite kings, but not so wise as Solomon. I gathered, too, that while he was in the Cage, he was often drunk; so the fault that has since, by all accounts, made such a wreck of him, had even then begun to show itself.

We were no sooner done eating than Cluny brought out an old, thumbed, greasy pack of cards, such as you might find in a mean inn; and his eyes brightened in his face as he proposed that we should fall to playing.

Now this was one of the things I had been brought up to eschew like disgrace; it being held by my father neither the part of a Christian nor yet of a gentleman to set his own livelihood and fish for that of others, on the cast of painted pasteboard. To be sure, I might have pleaded my fatigue, which was excuse enough; but I thought it behoved that I should bear a testimony. I must have got very red in the face, but I spoke steadily, and told him I had no call to be a judge of others, but for my own part, it was a matter in which I had no clearness.

Cluny stopped mingling the cards. "What in de'il name is this?" says he. "What kind of Whiggish, canting talk is this, for the house of Cluny Macpherson?"

"I will put my hand in the fire for Mr. Balfour," says Alan. "He is an honest and a mettle gentleman, and I would have ye bear in mind who says it. I bear a king's name," says he, cocking his hat: "and I and any that I call friend are company for the best. But the gentleman is tired and should sleep, if he has no mind to the cartes, it will never hinder you and me. And I'm fit and willing sir, to play ye any game that ye can name."

"Sir," said Cluny, "in this poor house of mine I would have you to ken that any gentleman may follow his pleasure. If your friend would like to stand on his head, he is welcome. And if either he, or you, or any other man, is not precisely satisfied, I will be proud to step outside with him."

I had no will that these two friends should cut their throats for my sake.

"Sir," said I, "I am very wearied, as Alan says; and what's more, as you are a man that likely has sons of your own, I may tell you it was a promise to my father."

"Say nae mair, say nae mair," said Cluny, and pointed me to a bed of heather in a corner of the Cage. For all that he was displeased enough, looked at me askance, and grumbled whem he looked. And indeed it must be owned that both my scruples and the words in which I declared them, smacked somewhat of the Covenanter, and were little in their place among wild Highland Jacobites.

What with the brandy and the venison, a strange heaviness had come over me; and I had scarce lain down upon the bed before I fell into a kind of trance, in which I continued almost the whole time of our stay in the Cage. Sometimes I was broad awake and understood what passed; sometimes I only heard voices, or men snoring, like the voice of a silly river; and the plaids upon the wall dwindled down and swelled out again, like firelight shadows on the roof. I must sometimes have spoken or cried out, for I remember I was now and then amazed at being answered; yet I was conscious of no particular nightmare, only of a general, black, abiding horror — a horror of the place I was in, and the bed I lay in, and the plaids on the wall, and the voices, and the fire, and myself.

The barber-gillie, who was a doctor too, was called in to prescribe for me; but as he spoke in the Gaelic, I understood not a word of his opinion, and was too sick even to ask for a translation. I knew well enough I was ill, and that was all I cared about.

I paid little heed while I lay in this poor pass. But Alan and Cluny were most of the time at the cards, and I am clear that Alan must have begun by winning; for I remember sitting up, and seeing them hard at it, and a great glittering pile of as much as sixty or a hundred guineas on the table. It looked strange enough, to see all this wealth in a nest upon a cliff-side, wattled about growing trees. And even then, I thought it seemed deep water for Alan to be riding, who had no better battle-horse than a green purse and a matter of five pounds.

The luck, it seems, changed on the second day. About noon I was wakened as usual for dinner, and as usual refused to eat, and was given a dram with some bitter infusion which the barber had prescribed. The sun was shining in at the open door of the Cage, and this dazzled and offended me. Cluny sat at the table, biting the pack of cards. Alan had stopped over the bed, and had his face close to my eyes; to which, troubled as they were with the fever, it seemed of the most shocking bigness.

He asked me for a loan of my money.

"What for?" said I.

"O, just for a loan," said he.

"But why?" I repeated. "I don't see."

"Hut, David!" said Alan, "ye wouldnae grudge me a loan?"

I would though, if I had had my sences! But all I thought of then was to get his face away, and I handed him my money.

On the morning of the third day, when we had been forty-eight hours in the Cage, I awoke with a great relief of spirits, very weak and weary indeed, but seing things of the right size and with their honest, everyday appearence. I had a mind to eat, moreover, rose from bed of my own movement, and as soon as we had breakfasted, stepped to the entry of the Cage and sat down outside in the top of the wood. It was a grey day with a cool, mild air; and I sat in a dream all morning, only disturbed by the passing by of Cluny's scouts and servants coming with provisions and reports; for as the coast was at that time clear, you might almost say he held court openly.

When I returned, he and Alan had laid the cards aside, and were questioning a gillie; and the chief turned about and spoke to me in the Gaelic.

"I have no Gaelic, sir," said I.

Now since the card question, everything I said or did had the power of annoying Cluny. "Your name has more sense than yourself, then," said he angrily; "for it's good Gaelic. But the point is this. My scout reports all clear in the south, and the question is, have ye the strength to go?"

I saw cards on the table, but no gold; only a heap of little written papers, and these all on Cluny's side. Alan, besides, had an odd look, like a man not very well content; and I began to have a strong misgiving.

"I do not know if I am as well as I should be," said I, looking at Alan; "but the little money we have has a long way to carry us."

Alan took his under-lip into his mouth, and looked upon the ground.

"David," says he at last, "I've lost it; there's the naked truth."

"My money too?" said I.

"Your money too," says Alan, with a groan, "Ye shouldnae have given it me. I'm daft when I get to the cartes."

"Hoot-toot! hoot-toot!" said Cluny. "It was all daffing; it's all nonsense. Of course you'll have your money back again, and the double of it, if ye'll make so free with me. It would be a singular thing for me to keep it. It's not to be supposed that I would be any hinderance to a gentleman in your situation; that would be a singular thing!" cries he, and began to pull gold out of his pocket with a mighty red face.

Alan said nothing, only looked on the ground.

"Will you step to the door with me, sir?" said I.

Cluny said he would be very glad, and followed me readily enough, but he looked flustered and put out.

"And now, sir," said I, "I must first acknowledge your generosity."

"Nonsensical nonsense!" cried Cluny. "Where's the generosity? This is just a most unfortunate affair; but what would ye have me do — boxed up in this beeskep of a cage of mine — but just set my friends to the cartes, when I can get them? And if they lose, of course, it's not to be supposed..." And here he came to a pause.

"Yes," said I, "if they lose, you give them back their money; and if they win, they carry away your in their pouches! I have said before that I grant your generosity; but to me, sir, it's a very painful thing to be placed in this position."

There was a little silence, in which Cluny seemed always as if he was about to speak, but said nothing. All the time he grew redder and redder in the face.

"I am a young man," said I, "and I ask your advice. Advise me as you would your son. My friend fairly lost this money, after having fairly gained a far greater sum of yours; can I accept it back again? Would that be the right part for me to play? Whatever I do, you can see for yourself it must be hard upon a man of any pride."

"It's rather hard on me, too, Mr. Balfour," said Cluny, "and ye give me very much the look of a man that has entrapped poor people to their hurt. I wouldnae have my friends come to any house of mine to accept affronts; no,"he cried, with a sudden heat of anger, "nor yet to give them!"

"And so you see, sir," said I, "there is something to be said upon my side; and this gambling is a very poor employ for gentlefolks. But I am still waiting your opinion."

I am sure if ever Cluny hated any man it was David Balfour. He looked me all over with a warlike eye, and I saw the challenge at his lips. But either my youth disarmed him, or perhaps his own sense of justice. Certainly it was a mortifying matter for all concerned, and not least for Cluny; the more credit that he took it as he did.

"Mr. Balfour," said he, "I think you are too nice and cove-
nanting, but for all that you have the spirit of a very pretty
gentleman. Upon my honest word, ye may take this money —
it's what I would tell my son — and here's my hand along
with it!"

CHAPTER XXIV

THE FLIGHT IN THE HEATHER: *THE QUARREL*

Alan and I were put across Loch Errocht under cloud of
night and went down its eastern shore to another hiding-
place near the head of Loch Rannoch, whither we were led
by one of the gillies of the Cage. This fellow carried all our
luggage and Alan's greatcoat in the bargain, trotting along
under the burthen, far less that the half of which used to
weigh me to the ground, like a stout hill pony with a feather;
yet he was a man that, in plain contest, I could have broken
on my knee.

Doubtless it was a great relief to walk disencumbered; and
perhaps without that relief, and the consequent sense of
liberty and lightness, I could not have walked at all. I was but
new risen from a bed of sickness; and there was nothing in
the state of our affairs to hearten me for much exertion;
travelling, as we did, over the most dismal deserts in Scotland
under a cloudy heaven, and with divided hearts among the
travellers.

For long, we said nothing; marching alongside or one
behind the other, each with a set countenance; I angry and
proud, and drawing what strength I had from these two
violent and sinful feelings; Alan angry and ashamed, ashamed
that he had lost my money, angry that I should take it so ill.

The thought of a separation ran always the stronger in my
mind; and the more I approved of it, the more ashamed I grew
of my approval. It would be a fine, handsome, generous thing,

indeed, for Alan to turn round and say to me: "Go, I am in the most danger, and my company only increases yours." But for me to turn to the friend who certainly loved me, and say to him: "You are in great danger, I am in but little; your friendship is a burden; go, take your risks and bear your hardships alone —" no, that was impossible; and even to think of it privily to myself, made my cheeks to burn.

And yet Alan had behaved like a child, and (what is worse) a treacherous child. Wheedling my money from me while I lay half-conscious was scarce better than theft; and yet he was trudging by my side, without a penny to his name, and by what I could see, quite blithe to sponge upon the money he had driven me to beg. True, I was ready to share it with him; but it made me rage to see him count upon my readiness.

These were the two things uppermost in my mind; and I could open my mouth upon neither without black ungenerosity. So I did the next worst, and said nothing, nor so much as looked once at my companion, save with the tail of my eye.

At last, upon the other side of Loch Errocht, going over a smooth, rushy place, where the walking was easy, he could bear it no longer, and came close to me.

"David," says he, "this is no way for two friends to take a small accident. I have to say that I'm sorry; and so that's said. And now if you have anything ye'd better say it."

"O," said I, "I have nothing."

He seemed disconcerted; at which I was meanly pleased.

"No," said he, with rather a trembling voice, "and you will bear me out that I have never reproached you."

"Never."

"Never," said he; "but ye ken very well that ye've done worse. Are we to part? Ye said so once before. Are ye to say it again? There's hills and heather enough between here and the two seas, David; and I will own I'm no very keen to stay where I'm not wanted."

This pierced me like a sword, and seemed to lay bare my private disloyalty.

"Alan Breck!" I cried; and then: "Do you think I am to turn my back on you in your chief need? You dursn't say it to my face. My whole counduct's there to give the lie to it. It's true I fell asleep upon the muir; but that was from weariness, and you do wrong to cast it up to me."

"Which is what I never did," said Alan.

"But aside from that," I continued, "what have I done that you should even me to the dogs by such a supposition? I never yet failed a friend, and it's not likely I'll begin with you. There are things between us that I can never forget, even if you can."

"I will only say this to ye David," said Alan, very quietly, "that I have long been owing ye my life, and now I owe ye money. Ye should try to make that burden light for me."

This ought to have touched me, and in a manner it did, but the wrong manner. I felt I was behaving badly; and was now not only angry with Alan, but angry with myself in the bargain; and it made me the more cruel.

"You asked me to speak," said I. "Well, then, I will. You own yourself that you have done me a dis-service; I have had to swallow an affront: I have never reproached you, I never named the thing till you did. And now you blame me," cried I, because I cannae laugh and sing as if I was glad to be affronted. The next thing will be that I'm to go down upon my knees and thank you for it! Ye should think more of others, Alan Breck. If ye thought more of others, ye would perhaps speak less about yourself; and when a friend that likes you very well has passed over an offence without a word, you would be blithe to let it lie, instead of making it a stick to break his back with. By your own way of it, it was you that was to blame; then it shouldnae be you to seek the quarrel."

"Aweel," said Alan, "say nae mair."

And we fell back into our former silence; and came to our journey's end, and supped, and lay down to sleep, without another word.

The gillie put us across Loch Rannoch in the dusk of the next day, and gave us his opinion as to our best route. This was to get us up at once into the tops of the mountains; to go round by a circuit, turning the heads of Glen Lyon, Glen Lochay, and Glen Dochart, and come down upon the lowlands by Kippen and the upper waters of the Forth. Alan was little pleased with a route that led us through the country of his bloodfoes, the Glenorchy Campbells. He objected that by turning to the east, we should come almost at once among the Athole Stewarts, a race of his own name and lineage although following a different chief, and came besides by a far easier and swifter way to the place whither we were bound. But the gillie, who was indeed the chief man of Cluny's scouts, had good reasons to give him on all hands, naming the force of troops in every district, and alleging finally (as well as I could understand) that we should nowhere be so little troubled as in a country of the Campbells.

Alan gave way at last, but with only half a heart. "It's one of the dowiest countries in Scotland," said he. „There's naething there that I ken, but heath, and crows, and Campbells. But I see that ye're a man of some penetration; and be it as ye please!"

We set forth accordingly by this itinerary; and for the best part of the three nights travelled on eerie mountains and among the well-heads of wild rivers; often buried in mist, almost continually blown and rained upon, and not once cheered by any glimpse of sunshine. By day, we lay and slept in the drenching hether; by night, incessantly clambered upon breakneck hills and among rude crags. We often wandered; we were often so involved in fog that we must lie quiet till it lightened. A fire was never to be thought of. Our only food

123

was drammach and a portion of cold meat that we had carried from the Cage; and as for drink, Heaven knows we had no want of water.

This was a dreadful time, rendered the more dreadful by the gloom of the weather and the country. I was never warm; my teeth chattered in my head; I was troubled with a very sore throat, such as I had on the isle; I had a painful stitch in my side, which never left me; and when I slept in my wet bed, with the rain beating above and the mud oozing below me, it was to live over again in fancy the worse part of my adventures — to see the tower of Shaws lit by lightning, Ransome carried below on the men's backs, Shuan dying on the roundhouse floor, or Colin Campbell grasping at the bosom of his coat. From such broken slumbers, I would be aroused in the gloaming, to sit up in the same puddle where I had slept, and sup cold drammach; the rain driving sharp in my face or running down my back in icy trickles; the mist enfolding us like as in a gloomy chamber — of, perhaps, if the wind blew, falling suddenly apart and showing us the gulf of some dark valley where the streams were crying aloud.

The sound of an infinite number of rivers came up from all round. In this steady rain the springs of the mountain were broken up; every glen gushed water like a cistern; every stream was in high spate, and had filled and overflowed its channel. During our night tramps, it was solemn to hear the voice of them below in the valleys, now booming like thunder now with an angry cry. I could well understand the story of the Water Kelpie, that demon of the streams, who is fabled to keep wailing, and roaring at the ford until the coming of the doomed traveller. Alan I saw believed it, or half believed it; and when the cry of the river rose more than usually sharp, I was little surprised (though, of curse, I would still be shocked) to see him cross himself in the manner of the Catholics.

During all these horrid wanderings we had no familiarity, scarcely even that of speech. The truth is that I was sickening for my grave, which is my best excuse. But besides that I was of an unforgiving disposition from my birth, slow to take offence, slower to forget it, and now incensed both against my companion and myself. For the best part of two days he was unweariedly kind; silent, indeed, but always ready to help, and always hoping (as I could very well see) that my displeasure would blow by. For the same lenght of time I stayed in myself, nursing my anger, roughly refusing his services, and passing him over with my eyes as if he had been a bush or a stone.

The second night, or rather the peep of the third day, found us upon a very open hill, so that we could not follow our usual plan, and lie down immediately to eat and sleep. Before we had reached a place of shelter, the grey had come pretty clear, for though it still rained, the clouds ran higher; and Alan, looking in my face, showed some marks of concern.

"Ye had better let me take your pack," said he, for perhaps the ninth time since we had parted from the scout beside Loch Rannoch.

"I do very well, I thank you," said I, as cold as ice.

Alan flushed darkly. "I'll not offer it again," he said. "I'm not a patient man, David."

"I never said you were," said I, which was exactly the rude, silly speech of a boy of ten.

Alan made no answer at the time, but his conduct answered for him. Henceforth, it is to be thought, he quite forgave himself for the affair at Cluny's; cocked his hat again, walked jauntily, whistled airs, and looked at me upon one side with a provoking smile.

The third night we were to pass through the western end of the country of Balquhidder. It came clear and cold, with a houch in the air like frost, and a northerly wind that blew the clouds away and made the stars bright. The streams were full, of course, and still made a great noise among the hills; but I observed that Alan thought no more upon the Kelpie, and was in high good spirits. As for me, the change of weather came too late; I had lain in the mire so long that (as the Bible has it) my very clothes "abhorred me;" I was dead weary, deadly sick and full of pains and shiverings; the chill of the wind went through me, and the sound of it confused my ears. In this poor state I had to bear from my companion something in the nature of a persecution. He spoke a good deal, and never without a taunt. "Whig" was the best name he had to give me. "Here," he would say, "here's a dub for ye to jump, my Whiggie! I ken you're a fine jumper!" And so on; all the time with a gibing voice and face.

I knew it was my own doing and no one else's; but I was too miserable to repent. I felt I could drag myself but a little farther; pretty soon, I must lie down and die on these wet mountains like a sheep or a fox, and my bones must whiten there like the bones of a beast. My head was light, perhaps; but I began to love the prospect, I began to glory in the thought of such a death, alone in the desert, with the wild eagles besieging my last moments. Alan would repent then, I thought; he would remember, when I was dead, how much he owed me, and the remembrance would be torture. So I went like a sick, silly, and bad-hearted schoolboy, feeding my anger against a fellow-man, when I would have been better on my knees, crying on God for mercy. And at each of Alan's taunts, I hugged myself. "Ah!" thinks I to myself, "I have a better taint in readiness; when I lie down and die, you will feel it like a buffet in your face; ah, what a revenge; ah, how you will regret your ingratitude and cruelty!"

All the while I was growing worse and worse. Once I had fallen, my legs simply doubling under me, and this had struck Alan for the moment; but I was affot so briskly, and set off again with such a natural manner, that he soon forgot the incident. Flushes of heat went over me, and then spasms of shuddering. The stitch in my side was hardly bearable. At last I began to feel that I could trail myself no further: and with that, there came on me all at once the wish to have it out with Alan, let my anger blaze, and be done with my life in a more sudden manner. He just called me "Whig." I stopped.

"Mr. Stewart," said I, in a voice that quivered like a fiddlestring, "you are older than I am, and should know your manners. Do you think it either very wise or very witty to cast any politics in my teeth? I thought, where folk differed, it was the part of gentlemen to differ civilly; and if I did not, I may tell you I could find a better taunt than some of yours."

Alan had stopped opposite to me, his hat cocked, his hands in his breeches pockets, his head a little on one side. He listened, smiling evilly, as I could see by the starlight; and when I had done he began to whistle a Jacobite air. It was the air made in mockery of General Cope's defeat at Preston Pans.

"Hey, Johnnie Cope, are ye waukin' yet?"

"And are your drums a-beatin' yet?"

And it came in my mind that Alan, on the day of that battle had been engaged upon the royal side.

"Why do ye take that air, Mr. Stewart?" said I. "Is that to remind me you have been beaten on both sides?"

The air stopped on Alan's lips. "David!" said he.

"But it's time these manners ceased," I continued; "and I mean you shall henceforth speak civilly of my King and my good friends the Campbells."

"I am a Stewart —" began Alan.

"O !" says I, "I ken ye bear a king's name. But you are to remember, since I have been in the Highlands, I have seen a good many of those that bear it; and the best I can say of them is this, that they would be none the worse of washing."

"Do you know that you insult me?" said Alan, very low.

"I am sorry for that," said I, "for I am not done; and if you distaste the sermon, I doubt another will please you as little. You have been chased in the field by the grown men of my party; it seems a poor kind of pleasure to outface a boy. Both the Campbells and the Whigs have beaten you; you have run before them like a hare. It behoves you to speak of them as of your betters."

Alan stood quite still, the tails of his greatcoat clapping behind him in the wind.

"This is a pity," he said at last. "There are things said that cannot be passed over."

"I never asked you to," said I. "I am as ready as yourself."

"Ready?" said he.

"Ready," I repeated, "I am no blower and boaster like some that I could name. Come on!" And drawing my sword, I fell on guard as Alan himself had taught me.

"David!" he cried. "Are ye daft? I cannae draw upon ye, David. It's fair murder."

"That was your look-out when you insulted me," said I.

"It's the truth!" cried Alan, and he stood for a moment, wringing his mouth in his hand like a man in sore perplexity.

"It's the bare truth," he said, and drew his sword. But before I could touch his blade with mine, he had thrown it from him and fallen to the ground.

"Na, na," he kept saying, "na, na — I cannae, I cannae."

At this the last of my anger oozed all out of me; and I found myself only sick, and sorry, and blank, and wondering at myself. I would have given the world to take back what I had said; but a word once spoken who can recapture? I minded me of all Alan's kindness and courage in the past, how he had helped and cheered and borne with me in our evil days; and then recalled my own insults, and saw that

I had lost for ever that doughty friend. At the same time, the sickness that hung upon me seemed to redouble, and the pang in my side was like a sword for sharpness. I thought I must have swooned where I stood.

This it was that gave me a thought. No apology could blot out what I had said; it was needless to think of one, none could cover the offence; but where an apology was vain, a mere cry for help might bring Alan back to my side. I put my pride away from me. "Alan!" I said; "if you cannae help me, I must just die here."

He started up sitting, and looked at me.

"It's true," said I. "I'm by with it. O, let me get into a house — I'll can die there easier." I had no need to pretend; whether I chose or not, I spoke in a waurning voice that would have melted a heart of stone.

"Can ye walk?" asked Alan.

"No," said I, "not without help. The last hour my legs have been fainting under me; I've a stitch in my side like a red-hot iron; I cannae breathe right. If I die, ye'll can forgive me, Alan? In my heart I like ye fine — even when I was the angriest."

"Wheesht, wheesht!" cried Alan. "Dinna say that! David, man, ye ken —" He shut his mouth upon a sob. "Let me get my arm about ye," he continued; "that's the way! Now lean upon me hard. Gude kens where there's a house ! We're in Balquhidder, too; there should be no want of houses, no, nor friends' houses here. Do ye gang easier so, David ?"

"Ay," said I, "I can be doing this way;" and I pressed his arm with my hand.

Again he came near sobbing. "Davie," said he, "I'm no a right man at all; I have neither sense nor kindness; I couldnae remember ye were just a bairn, I couldnae see ye were dying on your feet; Davie, ye'll have to try and forgive me."

129

"O, man, let's say no more about it!" said I. "We're neither one of us to mend the other — that's the truth! We must just bear and forbear, man, Alan. O, but my stitch is sore! Is there nae house?"

"I'll find a house to ye, David," he said stoutly. "We'll follow down the burn, where there's bound to be houses. My poor man, will ye no be better on my back?"

"O, Alan," says I, "and me a good twelve inches taller?"

"Ye're no such a thing," cried Alan, with a start. "There may be a trifling matter of an inch or two; I'm no saying I'm just exactly what you would call a tall man, whatever; and I dare say," he added, his voice taling off in a laughable manner, "now when I come to think of it, I dare say ye'll be just about right. Ay, it'll be a foot, or near hand; or may be even mair!"

It was sweet and laughable to hear Alan eat his words up in the fear of some fresh quarrel. I could have laughed, had not my stitch caught me so hard; but if I had laughed, I think I must have wept to.

"Alan," cried I, "what makes ye so good to me? What makes ye care for such a thankless fellow?"

"Deed, and I don't know," said Alan, "for just precisely what I though I liked about ye, was that ye never quarreled — and now I like ye better!"

CHAPTER XXV

IN BALQUHIDDER

At the door of the first house we came to, Alan knocked, which was no very safe enterprise in such a part of the Highlands as the Braes of Balquhidder. No great clan held rule there; it was filled and disputed by smal sects, and broken remnants, and what they call "chiefless folk," driven into the wild country about the springs of Forth and Teith by the advance of the Campbells. Here were Stewarts and Maclarens, which came to the same thing, for the Maclarens followed Alan's chief in war, and made but one clan with Appin. Here, too were many of the old, proscribed, nameless, red-handed clan of the Macgregors. They had always been ill-considered, and now worse than ever, having credit with no side or party in the whole country of Scotland. Their chief, Macgregor of Macgregor, was in exile; the more immediate leader of that part of them about Balquhidder, James More, Rob Roy's eldest son, lay waiting his trial in Edinburgh Castle; they were in ill-blood with Highlander and Lowlander, with the Grahames, the Maclarens, and the Stewarts; and Alan, who took up the quarrel of any friend, however distant, was extremely wishful to avoid them.

Chance served us very well; for it was a household of Maclarens that we found, where Alan was not only welcome for his name's sake, but known by reputation. Here then I was got to bed without delay, and a doctor fetched, who found me in a sorry plight. But whether because he was a very good doctor, or I a very young, strong man, I lay bedridden for no more than a week, and before a month I was able to take the road again with a good heart.

All this time Alan would not leave me though I often pressed him, and indeed his foolhardiness in staying was a common subject of outcry with the two or three friends that were let into the secret. He hid by day in a hole of the braes under a little wood; and at night, when the coast was clear, would come into the house to visit me. I need not say if I was pleased to see him. Mrs. Maclaren, our hostess, thought nothing good enough of such a guest; and as Duncan Dhu (which was the name of our host) had a pair of pipes in his house, and was much of a lover of music, the time of my recovery was quite a festival, and we commonly turned night into day.

The soldiers let us be; although once a party of two companies and some dragoons went by in the bottom of the valley, where I could see them through the window as I lay in bed. What was much more astonishing, no magistrate came near me, and there was no question put of whence I came or whither I was going, and in that time of excitement, I was as free of all inquiry as though I had lain in a desert. Yet my presence was known before I left to all the people in Balquhidder and the adjacent parts; many coming about the house on visits, and these (after the custom of the country) spreading the news among their neighbours. The bills, too, had now been printed. There was one pinned near the foot of my bed, where I could read my own not very flattering portrait and in larger characters, the amount of the blood money that had been set upon my life. Duncan Dhu and the rest that knew I had come there in Alan's company could have entertained no doubt of who I was; and many others must have had their guess. For though I had changed my clothes, I could not change my age or person; and Lowland boys of eighteen were not so rife in these parts of the world, and above all about that time, that they could fail to put one thing with another, and connect me with the bill. So it was, at least. Other folk keep a secret among two or three near friends, and somehow it leaks out, but among these clansmen, it is told to a whole countryside, and they will keep if for a century.

There was but one thing happened worth narrating; and that is the visit I had of Robin Oig, one of the sons of the notorious Rob Roy. He was sought upon all sides on a charge of carrying a young woman from Balfron and marrying her (as was alleged) by force; yet he stepped about Balquhidder like a gentleman in his own walled policy. It was he who had shot James Maclaren at the plough stilts, a quarrel never satisfied; yet he walked into the house of his blood enemies as a rider might into a public inn.

Duncan had time to pass me word of who he was; and looked at one another in concern. You should understand, it was then close upon the time of Alan's coming; the two were little likely to agree; and yet if we sent word or sought to make a signal, it was sure to arouse suspicion in a man under so dark a cloud as the Macgregor.

He came in with a great show of civility, but like a man among inferiors; took off his bonnet to Mrs. Maclaren, but clapped it on his head again to speak to Duncan; and having thus set himself (as he would have thought) in a proper light, came to my bedside and bowed.

"I am given to know, sir," said he "that your name is Balfour."

"They call me David Balfour." said I, "at your service."

"I would give ye my name in return, sir," he replied, "but it's one somewhat blown upon of late days; and it'll perhaps suffice if I tell ye that I am own brother to James More Drummond or Macgregor, of whom ye will scarce have failed to hear."

"No, sir," said I, a little alarmed; "nor yet of your father, Macgregor-Campbell." And I sat up and bowed in bed; for I thought best to compliment him, in case he was proud of having had an outlaw to his father.

He bowed in return. "But what I am come to say, sir," he went on, "is this. In the year '45, my brother raised a part of the 'Gregara', and marched six companies to strike a stroke for the good side; and the surgeon that marched with our clan and cured my brother's leg when it was broken in the brush at Preston Pans, was a gentleman of the same name precisely as yourself. He was brother to

Balfour of Baith; and if you are in any reasonable degree of nearness one of that gentleman's kin, I have come to put myself and my people at your command."

You are to remember that I knew no more of my descent than any cadger's dog; my uncle, to be sure, had prated of some of our high connections, but nothing to the present purpose; and there was nothing left me but that bitter disgrace of owning that I could not tell.

Robin told me shortly he was sorry he had put himself about, turned his back upon me without a sign of salutation, and as he went towards the door, I could hear him telling Duncan that I was "only some kinless loon that didn't know his own father." Angry as I was at these words, and ashamed of my own ignorance, I could scarce keep from smiling that a man who was under the lash of the law (and was indeed hanged some three years later) should be so nice as to the descent of his acquaintances.

Just in the door, we heard Alan coming in; and the two drew back and looked at each other like strange dogs. They were neither of them big men, but they seemed fairly to swell out with pride. Each wore a sword, and by a movement of his haunch, thrust clear the hilt of it, so that it might be the more readily grasped and the blade drawn.

"Mr. Stewart, I am thinking," says Robin.

"Troth, Mr. Macgregor, it's not a name to be ashamed of", answered Alan.

"I did not know ye were in my country, sir," says Robin.

"It sticks in my mind that I am in the country of my friends the Maclarens," says Alan.

"That's a kittle point," returned the other, "there may be two words to say to that. But I think I will have heard that you are a man of your sword?"

"Unless ye were born deaf, Mr. Macgregor, ye will have heard a good deal more than that," says Alan. "I am not the only man that can draw steel in Appin; and when my kinsman and captain, Ardshiel, had a talk with a gentleman of your name, not so many years back, I could never hear that the Macgregor had the best of it."

"Do ye mean my father, sir?" says Robin.

"Well, I wouldnae wonder," said Alan. "The gentleman I have in my mind had the ill'taste to clap Campbell to his name."

"I was thinking that," said Robin.

I was half out of bed, and Duncan had been hanging at the elbow of these fighting-cocks, ready to intervene upon the least occasion. But when that word was uttered, it was a case of now or never; and Duncan, with something of a white face to be sure, thrust himself between.

"Gentlemen," said he, "I will have been thinking of a very different matter whateffer. Here are my pipes, and here are you two gentlemen who are baith acclaimed pipers. It's an auld dispute which one of ye's the best. Here will be a braw chance to settle it."

"Why, sir," said Alan, still addressing Robin, from whom indeed he had not so much as shifted his eyes, not yet Robin from him, "why, sir," says Alan, "I think I will have heard some rumour of the sort. Have ye music, as folk say? Are ye a bit of a piper?"

"I can pipe like a Macrimmon!" cries Robin.

"And that is a very bold word," quoth Alan.

"I have made bolder words good before now," returned Robin, "and that against better adversaries."

"It's easy to try that," says Alan.

Duncan Dhu made haste to bring out the pair of pipes that was his principal possession, and to set before his guests a mutton-ham and a bottle of that drink which they call

Athole brose, and which is made of old whisky, strained honey, and sweet cream, slowly beaten together in the right order and proportion. The two enemies were still on the very breach of a quarrel; but down they sat, one upon each side of the peat fire, with a mighty show of politeness. Maclaren pressed them to taste his mutton-ham and the wife's brose, reminding them the wife was out of Athole and had a name far and wide for her skill in that confection. But Robin put aside these hospitalities as bad for the breath.

"I would have ye to remark, sir," said Alan, "that I have-n'ae broken bread for near upon ten hours, which will be worse for the breath than any brose in Scotland."

"I will take no advantages, Mr. Stewart," replied Robin. "Eat and drink; I'll follow you."

Each ate a small portion of the ham and drank a glass of the brose to Mrs. Maclaren; and then after a great number of civilities, Robin took the pipes and played a little spring in a very ranting manner.

"Ay, ye can blow," said Alan; and taking the instrument from his rival, he first played the same spring in a manner identical with Robin's; and then wandered into variations, which, as he went on, he decorated with a perfect flight of grace-notes, such as pipers love, and call the "warblers."

I had been pleased with Robin's playing, Alan's ravished me.

"That's no very bad, Mr. Stewart," said the rival, "but ye show a poor device in your warblers."

"Me!" cried Alan the blood starting to his face. "I give ye the lie."

"Do ye own yourself beaten at the pipes, then," cried Robin, "that ye seek to change them for the sword?"

"And that's very well said, Mr. Macgregor," returned Alan; "and in the meantime" (laying a strong accent on the word), "I take back the lie. I appeal to Duncan."

"Indeed, ye need appeal to naebody," said Robin. "Ye're a far better judge than any Maclaren in Balquhidder: for it's a God's truth that you're a very creditable piper for a Stewart. Hand me the pipes."

Alan did as he asked; and Robin proceeded to imitate and correct some part of Alan's variations, which it seemed that he remembered perfectly.

"Ay, ye have music," said Alan gloomily.

"And now be the judge yourself, Mr. Stewart," said Robin; and taking up the variations from the beginning, he worked them throughout to so new a purpose, with such ingenuity and sentiment, and with so odd a fancy and so quick a knack in the gracenotes, that I was amazed to hear him.

As for Alan, his face grew dark and hot, and he sat and gnawed his fingers, like a man under some deep affront. "Enough!" he cried. "Ye can blow the pipes — make the most of that." And he made as if to rise.

But Robin only held out his hand as if to ask for silence and struck into the slow measure of a pibroch. It was a fine piece of music in itself, and nobly played; but it seems, besides, it was a piece peculiar to the Appin Stewarts and a chief favourite with Alan. The first notes were scarce out, before there came a change in his face; when the time quickened, he seemed to grow restless in his seat; and long before that piece was at an end, the last signs of his anger died from him, and he had no thought but for the music.

"Robin Oig," he said, when it was done, "ye are a great piper. I'm not fit to blow in the same kingdom with ye. Body of me! ye had mair music in your sporran than I have in my head! And though it still sticks in my mind that I could maybe show ye another of it with the cold steel, I warn ye beforehand — it'll no be fair! It would go against my heart to haggle a man that can blow the pipes as you can!"

Thereupon the quarrel was made up; all night long the brose was going and the pipes changing hands; and the day had come pretty bright, and the three men were none the better for what they had been taking, before Robin as much as thought upon the road.

CHAPTER XXVI

END OF THE FLIGHT :
WE PASS THE FORTH

The month, as I have said, was not yet out, but it was already far through August, and beautiful warm weather, with every sign of an early and great harvest, when I was pronounced able for my journey. Our money was now run to so low an ebb that we must think first of all on speed; for if we came not soon to Mr. Rankeillor's, or if when we came there he should fail to help me, we must surely starve. In Alan's view, besides, the hunt must have now greatly slackened; and the line of the Forth and even Stirling Bridge, which is the main pass over the river, would be watched with little interest.

"It's a chief principle in military affairs," said he, "to go where ye are least expected. Forth is our trouble; ye ken the saying 'Forth bridles the Wild Hielandman'. Well, if we seek to creep round about the head of that river and come down by Kippen or Balfron, it's just precisely there that they'll be looking to lay hands on us. But if we stave on straight to the auld Brig of Stirling, I'll lay my sword they let us pass unchallenged."

The first night, accordingly, we pushed to the house of a Maclaren in Strathire, a friend of Duncan's, where we slept the twenty-first of the month, and whence we set forth again about the fall of night to make another easy stage. The twenty-second we lay in a heather bush on the hillside in Uam Var, within view of a herd of deer, the happiest ten hours of sleep in a fine, breathing sunshine and on bonedry ground, that I have ever tasted. That night we struck Allan Water, and followed it down; and coming to the edge of the hills saw the whole Carse of Stirling underfoot, as flat as a pancake, with the town and castle on a hill in the midst of it, and the moon shining on the Links of Forth.

"Now," said Alan, "I kenna if ye care, but ye're in your own land again. We passed the Hieland Line in the first hour; and now if we could but pass yon crooked water, we might cast our bonnets in the air."

In Allan Water, near by where it falls into the Forth, we found a little sandy islet, overgrown with burdock, butterbur, and the like low plants that would just cover us if we lay flat. Here it was we made our camp, within plain view of Stirling Castle, whence we could hear the drums beat as some part of the garrison paraded. Shearers worked all day in a field on one side of the river, and we could hear the stones going on the hooks and the voices and even the words of the men talking. It behoved to lie close and keep silent. But the sand of the little isle was sun-warm, the green plants gave us shelter for our heads, we had food and drink in plenty; and to crown all, we were within sight of safety.

As soon as the shearers quit their work and the dusk began to fall, we waded ashore and struck for the Brigde of Stirling, keeping to the fields and under the field fences.

The brigde is close under the castle hill, an old, high narrow bridge with pinnacles along the parapet; and you may conceive with how much interest I looked upon it, not only as a place famous in history, but as the very doors of salvation to Alan and myself. The moon was not yet up when we came there; a few lights shone along the front of the fortress, and lower down a few lighted windows in the town; but it was all mighty still, and there seemed to be no guard upon the passage.

I was for pushing straight across; but Alan was more wary.

"It looks unco' quiet," said he; "but for all that we'll lie down here cannily behind a dyke, and make sure."

So we lay for about a quarter of an hour, whiles whispering, whiles lying still and hearing nothing earthly but the washing of the water on the piers. At last came by an old, hobbling woman with a crutch stick; who first stopped a little, close to where we lay, and bemoaned herself and the long way she had travelled; and then set forth again up the steep spring of the bridge. The woman was so little, and the night still so dark, that we soon lost sight of her; only heard the sound of her steps, and her stick, and a cough that she had by fits, draw slowly farther away.

"She's bound to be across now," I whispered.

"Na," said Alan, "her foot still sounds hollow upon the bridge."

And just then — "Who goes?" cried a voice, and we heard the butt of a musket rattle on the stones. I must suppose the sentry had been sleeping, so that had we tried, we might have passed unseen; but he was awake now, and the chance forfeited.

"This'll never do," said Alan. "This'll never, never do for us, David."

And without another word, he began to crawl away through the fields; and a little after, being well out of eyeshot, got to his feet again, and struck along a road that led to the eastward. I could not conceive what he was doing; and indeed I was so sharply cut by the disappointment, that I was little likely to be pleased with anything. A moment back and I had seen myself knocking at Mr. Rankeillor's door to claim my inheritance, like a hero in a ballad; and here was I back again, a wandering, hunted blackguard, on the wrong side of the Forth.

"Well?" said I.

"Well," said Alan, "what would ye have? They're none such fools as I took them for. We have still the Forth to pass, Davie — weary fall the rains that fed and the hillsides that guided it!"

"And why go east?" said I.

"Ou, just upon the chance!" said he. "If we cannae pass the river, we'll have to see what we can do for the firth."

"There are fords upon the river, and none upon the firth," said I.

"To be sure there are fords, and a bridge forbye," quoth Alan; "and of what service, when they are watched?"

"Well," said I, "but a river can be swum."

"By them that have the skill of it," returned he; "but I have yet to hear that either you or me is much of a hand at that exercise; and for my own part, I swim like a stone."

"I'm not up to you in talking back, Alan," I said; "but I can see we're making bad worse. If it's hard to pass a river, it stands to reason it must be worse to pass a sea."

"But there's such a thing as a boat," says Alan, "or I'm the more deceived."

"Ay, and such a thing as money," said I. "But for us that have neither one nor other, they might just as well not have been invented."

"Ye thing so?" said Alan.

"I do that," said I.

"David," says he, "ye're a man of small invention and less faith. But let me set my wits upon the hone, and if I cannae beg, borrow, nor yet steal a boat, I'll make one!"

I think I see ye!" said I. "And what's more than all that: if ye pass a bridge, it can tell no tales; but if we pass the firth, there's the boat on the wrong side — somebody must have brought it — the countryside will be all in a bizz —"

"Man!" cried Alan, "if I make a boat, I'll make a body to take it back again! So leave me with no more of your nonsense, but walk (for that's what you've go to do) and let Alan think for ye."

All night, then, we walked through the north side of the Carse, under the high line of the Ochil mountains; and by Alloa and Clackmannan and Culross, all of which we avoided: and about ten in the morning, mighty hungary and tired, came to the little clachan of Limekilns. This is a place that sits near in by the waterside, and looks across the Hope to the town of Queen's Ferry. Smoke went up from both of these, and from other villages and farms upon all hands. The fields were being reaped; two ships lay anchored, and boats were coming and going on the Hope. It was altogether a right pleasant sight to me; and I could not take my fill of gazing at these comfortable, green, cultivated hills and the busy people both of the field and sea.

For all that, there was Mr. Rankeillor's house on the south shore, where I had no doubt wealth awaited me; and here was I upon the north, clad in poor enough attire of an outlandish fashion, with three silver shilling left to me of all my fortune, a price set upon my head, and an outlawed man for my sole company.

"O, Alan!" said I, "to think of it! Over there, there's all that heart could want waiting me; and the birds go over, and the boats go over — all that please can go, but just me only! O, man, but it's a heartbreak!"

In Limekilns we entered a small change-house, which we only knew to be a public by the wand over the door, and bought some bread and cheese from a good-looking lass

142

that was the servant. This we carried with us in a bundle, meaning to sit and eat it in a bush of wood on the sea-shore, that we saw some third part of a mile in front. As we went, I kept looking across the water and sighing to myself; and though I took no heed of it, Alan had fallen into a muse. At last he stopped in the way.

"Did ye take heed of the lass we bought this of?" says he, tapping on the bread and cheese.

"To be sure," said I, "and a bonny lass she was."

"Ye thought that?" cries he. "Man, David, that's good news."

"In the name of all that's wonderful, why so?" says I. "What good can that do?"

"Well," said Alan, with one of his droll looks, "I was rather in hopes it would maybe get us that boat."

"If it were the other way about, it would be liker it," said I.

"That's all that you ken, ye see," said Alan. "I don't want the lass to fall in love with ye, I want her to be sorry for ye, David; to which end there is no manner of need that she should take for a beauty. Let me see" (looking me curiously over), "I wish ye were a wee thing paler; but, apart from that, ye'll do fine for my purpose — ye have a fine, hand-dog, rag-and-tatter, clappermaclaw kind of look to ye, as if ye had stolen the coat from a potatobogle. Come; right about and back to the change-house for that boat of ours."

I followed him, laughing.

"David Balfour," said he, "ye're a very funny gentleman by your way of it, and this is a funny employ for ye, no doubt. For all that, if ye have any affection for my neck (to say nothing of your own) ye will perhaps be kind enough to take this matter responsibly. I am going to do a bit of playacting, the bottom ground of which is just exactly as serious as the gallows for the pair of us. So bear it, if ye please, in mind, and conduct yourself according."

"Well, well," said I, "have it as you will."

As we got near the clachan, he made me take his arm and hang upon it like one almost helpless with weariness; and by the time he pushed open the change-house door, he seemed to be half-carrying me. The maid appeared surprised (as well she might be) at our speedy return ; but Alan had no words to spare for her in explanation, helped me to a chair, called for a tass of brandy, with which he fed me in little sips, and then breaking up the bread and cheese helped me to eat it like a nursery-lass ; the whole with that grave, concerned, affectionate countenance, that might have imposed upon a judge. It was small wonder if the maid were taken with the picture we presented, of a poor, sick, overwrought lad and his most tender comrade. She drew quite near, and stood leaning with her back on the next table.

"What's like wrong with him?" said she at last.

Alan turned upon her, to my great wonder, with a kind of fury. "Wrong?" cried he. "He's walked more hundreds of miles than he has hairs upon his chin, and slept oftener in wet heather than dry sheets. Wrong, quo' she! Wrong enough, I would think! Wrong, indeed!" and he kept grumbling to himself, as he fed me, like a man ill-pleased.

"He's young for the like of that," said the maid.

"Over young," said Alan, with his back to her.

"He would be better riding,' says she.

"And where could I get a horse to him?" cried Alan, turning on her with the same appearance of fury. "Would ye have me steal?"

I thought that this roughness would have sent her off in dudgeon, as indeed it closed her mouth for the time.

But my companion knew very well what he was doing; and for as simple as he was in some things of life, had a great fund of roguishness in such affairs as these.

"Ye neednae tell me," she said at last — "ye're gentry."

"Well," said Alan, softened a little (I believe against his will) by this artless comment, "and suppose we were? Did ever you hear that gentrice put money in folk's pockets?"

She sighed at this, as if she were herself some disinherited great lady. "No," says she, "that's true indeed."

I was all this while chafing at the part I played, and sitting tongue tied between shame and merriment; but somehow at this I could hold in no longer, and bade Alan let me be, for I was better already. My voice stuck in my throat, for I ever hated to take part in lies; but my very embarrassment helped on the plot for the lass no doubt set down my husky voice to sickness and fatigue.

"Has he nae friends?" she said, in a tearful voice.

"That has he so!" cried Alan, "if we could but win to them! — friends and rich friends, beds to lie in, food to eat, doctors to see to him — and here he must tramp in the dubs and sleep in the heather like a beggarman."

"And why that?" says the lass.

"My dear," said Alan, "I cannae very safely say; but I'll tell ye what I'll do instead," says he, "I'll whistle ye a bit tune." And with that he leaned pretty far over the table, and in a mere breath of a whistle, but with a wonderful pretty sentiment, gave her a few bars of "Charlie is my darling."

"Wheesht," said she, and looked over her shoulder to the door.

"That's it," said Alan.

"And him so young!" cries the lass.

"He's old enough to —" and Alan struck his forefinger on the back of his neck, meaning that I was old enough to lose my head.

"It would be a black shame," she cried, flushing high.

"It's what will be, though," said Alan, "unless we manage the better."

At this the lass turned and ran out of that part of the house, leaving us alone together. Alan in high good humour at the furthering of his schemes, and I in bitter dudgeon at being called a Jacobite and treated like a child.

"Alan," I cried, "I can stand no more of this!"

"Ye'll have to sit it then, Davie," said he. "For if ye upset the pot now, ye may scrape your own life out of the fire, but Alan Breck is a dead man."

This was so true that I could only groan; and even my groan served Alan's purpose, for it was overheard by the lass as she came flying in again with a dish of white puddings and a bottle of strong ale.

"Poor lamb!" says she, and had no sooner set the meat before us, that she touched me on the shoulder with a little friendly touch, as much as to bid me cheer up. Then she told us to fall to, and there would be no more to pay; for the inn was her own, or at least her father's, and he was gone for the day to Pittencrieff. We waited for no second bidding, for bread and cheese is but cold comfort and the puddings smelt excellently well; and while we sat and ate, she took up that same place by the next table, looking on, and thinking, and frowning to herself, and drawing the string of her apron through her hand.

"I'm thinking ye have rather a long tongue," she said at last to Alan.

"Ay," said Alan; "but ye see I ken the folk I speak to."

"I would never betray ye," said she, "if ye mean that."

"No," said he, "ye're not that kind. But I'll tell ye what ye would do, ye would help."

"I couldnae," said she, shaking her head. "Na, I couldnae."

"No," said he, "but if ye could?"

She answered him nothing.

"Look here, my lass," said Alan, "there are boats in the kingdom of Fife, for I saw two (no less) upon the beach, as I came in by your town's end. Now if we could have the use of a boat to pass under a cloud of night into Lothian, and some secret, decent kind of a man to bring that boat back again and keep his counsel, there would be two souls saved — mine to all likelihood   his to a dead surety. If we lack the boat, we have but three shillings left in this wide world; and where to go, and how to do, and what other place there is for us except the chains of a gibbet I give you my naked word, I kenna! Shall we go wanting, lassie? Are ye to lie in your warm bed and think upon us, when the wind gowls in the chimney and the rain trills on the roof? Are ye to eat your meat by the cheeks of a red fire, and think upon this poor sick lad of mine, biting his finger-ends on a blae muir for cauld and hunger? Sick or sound, he must aye be moving; with the death grapple at his throat he must aye be trailing in the rain on the long roads; and when he gants his last on a rickle of cauld stanes, there will be nae friends near him but only me and God."

At this appeal I could see the lass was in great trouble of mind, being tempted to help us, and yet in some fear she might be helping malefactors; and so now I determined to step in myself and to allay her scruples with a portion of the truth.

"Did ever you hear," said I, "of Mr. Rankeillor of the Ferry?"

"Rankeillor the writer?" said she. "I daursay that!"

"Well," said I, "it's to his door that I am bound, so you may judge by that if I am an ill-doer; and I will tell you more, that though I am indeed, by a dreadful error, in some peril of my life, King George has no truer friend in all Scotland than myself."

Her face cleared up mightily at this, although Alan's darkened.

"That's more than I would ask," said she. "Mr. Rankeillor is a kent man." And she bade us finish our meat, get clear of the clachan as soon as might be, and lie close in the bit wood on the sea beach. "And ye can trust me," says she, "I'll find some means to put you over."

At this we waited for no more, but shook hands with her upon the bargain, made short work of the puddings, and set forth again from Limekilns as far as to the wood. It was a small piece of perhaps a score of elders and hawthorns and a few young ashes, not thick enough to veil us from passers-by upon the road or beach. Here we must lie, however, making the best of the brave warm weather and the good hopes we now had of a deliverance, and planning more particularly what remained for us to do.

We had but one trouble all day; when a strolling piper came and sat in the same wood with us; a rednosed, bleareyed, drunken dog, with a great bottle of whisky in his pocket, and a long story of wrongs that has been done him by all sorts of persons, from the Lord President of the Court of Session, who had denied him justice, down to the Baillies of Inverkeithing who had given him more of it than he desired. It was impossible but he should conceive some suspicion of two men lying all day concealed in a thicket and having no business to allege. As long as he stayed there, he kept us in hot water with prying questions, and after he was gone, as he was a man not very likely to hold his tongue, we were in the grater impatience to be gone ourselves.

The day came to an end with the same brightness; the night fell quiet and clear; lights came out in houses and hamlets, and then, one after another, began to be put out; but it was past eleven, and we were long since strangely tortured with anxieties before we heard the grinding of oars upon the rowingpins. At that, we looked out and saw the lass herself coming rowing to us in a boat. She had trusted no one with our affairs, not even her sweetheart, if she had one; but as soon as her father was asleep, had left the house by a window, stolen a neighbour's boat, and come to our assistance single-handed.

I was abashed how to find expression for my thanks; but she was no less abashed at the thought of hearing them; begged us to lose no time and to hold our peace, saying (very properly) that the heart of our matter was in haste and silence ; and so, what with one thing and another, she had set us on the Lothian shore not far from Garriden, had shaken hands with us, and was out again at sea and rowing for Limekilns, before there was one word said either of her service or our gratitude.

Even after she was gone, we had nothing to say, as indeed nothing was enough for such a kindness. Only Alan stood a great while upon the shore shaking his head.

"It is a very fine lass," he said at last. "David, it is a very fine lass." And a matter of an hour later, as we were lying in a den on the sea-shore and I had been already dozing, he broke out again in commendations of her character. For my part, I could say nothing, she was so simple a creature that my heart smote me both with remorse and fear; remorse because we had traded upon her ignorance ; and fear lest we should have anyway involved her in the dangers of our situation.

CHAPTER XXVII

I COME TO MR. RANKEILLOR

The next day it was agreed that Alan should fend for himself till sunset ; but as soon as it began to grow dark, he should lie in the fields by the roadside near to Newhalls, and stir for naught until he heard me whistling. At first I proposed I should give him for a signal the "Bonnie House of Airlie," which was a favourite of mine; but he objected that as the piece was very commonly known, any ploughman might whistle it by accident; and taught me instead a little fragment of a Highland air, which has run in my head from that day to this, and will likely run in my head when I lie dying. Every time it comes to me, it takes me off to that last day of my uncertainty, with Alan sitting up in the bottom of the den, whistling and beating the measure with a finger and the grey of the dawn coming on his face.

I was in the long street of Queen's Ferry before the sun was up. It was a fairly built burgh, the houses of good stone many slated; the townhall not so fine, I thought, as that of Peebles, nor yet the street so noble; but take it altogether, it put me to shame for my foul tatters.

As the morning went on, and the fires to be kindled, and the windows to open, and the people to appear out of the houses, my concern and despondency grew ever the blacker. I saw now that I had no grounds to stand upon; and no clear proof of my rights, nor so much as of my own identity. If it was all a bubble, I was indeed sorely cheated and left in a sore pass. Even if things were as I conceived, it would in all likelihood take time to establish my contentions; and what time had I to spare with less than three shillings in my pocket, and a condemned hunted man upon my hands to ship out of the country? Truly, if my hope broke with me, it might come to the gallows yet for both of us. And as I continued to walk up and down, and saw people looking askance at me upon the street or out of windows, and nudging or speaking one to another with smiles, I began to take a fresh apprehension: that it might be no easy matter even to come to speech of the lawyer, far less to convince him of my story.

For the life of me I could not muster up the courage to address any of these reputable burghers; I thought shame even to speak with them in such a pickle of rags and dirt; and if I asked for the house of such a man as Mr. Rankeillor, I supposed they would have burst out laughing in my face. So I went up and down, and through the street, and down to the harbour-side, like a dog that has lost its master, with a strange gnawing in my inwards, and every now and then a movement of despair. It grew to be high day at last perhaps nine in the forennon; and I was worn with these wanderings, and chanced to have stopped in front of a very good house on the landward side, a house with beautiful, clear glass windows, flowering knots upon the sills, the walls new-harled, and a chasedog sitting yawning on the step like one that was at home. Well, I was even envying this dumb brute, when the door fell open and there issued forth a shrewd, ruddy, kindly, consequential man in a well-powdered wig and spectacles. I was in such a plight that no one set eyes upon me once but he looked at me again; and this gentleman, as it proved, was so much struck with my poor appearance that he came straight up to me and asked me what I did.

I told him I was come to the Queen's Ferry on business, and taking heart of grace, asked him to direct me to the house of Mr. Rankeillor.

"Why," said he, "that is his house that I have just come out of; and for a rather singural chance, I am that very man."

"Then, sir," said I, "I have to beg the favour of an interview."

"I do not know your name," said he, "nor yet your face."

"My name is David Balfour," said I.

"David Balfour?" he repeated, in rather a high tone, like one surprised. "And where have you come from, Mr. David Balfour?" he asked, looking me pretty dryly in the face.

"I have come from a great many strange places, sir," said I; "but I think it would be as well to tell you where and how in a moreprivate manner."

He seemed to muse awhile, holding his lip in his hand, and looking now at me and now upon the causeway of the street.

"Yes," says he, "that will be the best, no doubt." And he led me back with him into his house, cried out to some one whom I could not see that he would be engaged all morning, and brought me into a little dusty chamber full of books and documents. Here he sat down, and bade me be seated; though I thought he looked a little ruefully from his clean chair to my muddy rags. "And now," says he, "if you have any business, pray be brief and come swiftly to the point. NEC GEMINO BELLUM TROJANUM ORDITUR AB OVO — do you understand?' says he, with a keen look.

"I will even do as Horace says, sir," I answered, smiling, "and carry you IN MEDIAS RES." He nodded as if he was well pleased, and indeed his scrap of Latin had been set to test me. For all that, and though I was somewhat encouraged, the blood came in my face when I added: "I have reason to believe myself some rights on the estate of Shaws."

He got a paper book out of a drawer and set it before him open. "Well?" said he.

But I had shot my bolt and sat speechless.

"Come, come, Mr. Balfour," said he, "you must continue. Where were you born?"

"In Essendean, sir," said I, "year 1733, the 12th of March."

He seemed to follow this statement in his paper book; but what that meant I knew not. "Your father and mother?" said he.

"My father was Alexander Balfour, schoolmaster of that place," said I, "and my mother Grace Pittarrow; I think her people were from Angus."

"Have you any papers proving your identity?" asked Mr. Rankeillor.

"No, sir," said I, "but they are in the hands of Mr. Campbell, the minister, and could be readily produced. Mr. Campbell, too, would give me his word; and for that matter, I do not think my uncle would deny me."

"Meaning Mr. Ebenezer Balfour?" says he.

"The same," said I.

"Who did see you?" asked he.

"By whom I was received into his own house," I answered.

"Did you ever meet a man of the name of Hoseason?" asked Mr. Rankeillor.

"I did so, sir, for my sins," said I; "for it was by his means and the procurement of my uncle, that I was kidnapped within sight of this town, carried to sea, suffered shipwreck and a hundred other hardships, and stand before you to-day in this poor accoutrement."

"You say you were shipwrecked," said Rankeillor; "where was that?"

"Off the south end of the Isle of Mull," said I. "The name of the isle on which I was cast up is the Island Earraid."

"Ah!" says he, smiling, "you are deeper than me in the geography. But so far, I may tell you, this agrees pretty exactly with other information that I hold. But you say you were kidnapped; in what sense?"

"In the plain meaning of the word, sir," said I. "I was on my way to your house, when I was trepanned on board the brig, cruelly struck down, thrown below, and knew no more of any thing till we were far at sea. I was destined for the plantations; a fate that, in God's providence, I have escaped."

"The brig was lost on June the 27th," says he, looking in his book, "and we are now at August the 24th. Here is a considerable hiatus, Mr. Balfour, of near upon two months. It has already caused a vast amount of trouble to your friends; and I own I shall not be very well contented until it is set right."

"Indeed, sir," said I, "these months are very easily filled up; but yet before I told my story, I would be glad to know that I was talking to a friend."

"This is to argue in a circle," said the lawyer. "I cannot be convinced till I have heard you. I cannot be your friend till I am properly informed. If you were more trustful, it would better befit your time of life. And you know, Mr. Balfour, we have a proverb in the country that evil-doers are aye evil-dreaders."

"You are not to forget, sir," said I, "that I have already suffered by my trustfulness; and was shipped off to be a slave by the very man that (if I rightly understand) is your employer."

All this while I had been gaining ground with Mr. Rankeillor and in proportion as I gained ground, gaining confidence. But at this sally, which I made with something of a smile myself, he fairly laughed aloud.

"No, no," said he, "it is not so bad as that. FUI NIN SUM. I WAS indeed your uncle's man of business; but while you (IMBERIS JUVENIS CUSTODE REMOTO) were gallivanting in the west, a good deal of water has run under the bridges; and if your ears did not sing, it was not for lack of being talked about. On the very day of your sea disaster, Mr. Campbell stalked into my office, demanding you from all the winds. I had never heard of your existence;

154

but I had known your father; and from matters in my competence (to be touched upon hereafter) I was disposed to fear the worst. Mr. Ebenezer admitted having seen you; declared (what seemed improbable) that he had given you considerable sums; and you had started for the continent of Europe intending to fulfil your education, which was probable and praiseworthy. Interrogated how you had come to send no word to Mr. Campbell, he deponed that you had expressed a great desire to break with your past life. Further interrogated where you were now, protested ignorance, but believed you were in Leyden. That is a close sum of his replies. I am not exactly sure that any one believed him," continued Mr. Rankeillor with a smile; "and in particular he so much disrelished some expressions of mine that (in a word) he showed me to the door. We were then at a full stand; for whatever shrewd suspicions we might entertain, we had no shadow of probation. In the very article, comes Captain Hoseason with the story of your drowning; whereupon all fell through; with no consequences but concern to Mr. Campbell, injury to my pocket, and another blot upon your uncle's character, which could ill-afford it. And now Mr. Balfour," said he, "you understand the whole process of these matters, and can judge for yourself to what extent I may be trusted."

Indeed he was more pedantic than I can represent him, and placed more scraps of Latin in his speech; but it was all uttered with a fine geniality of eye and manner which went far to conquer my distrust. Moreover I could see he now treated me as if I was myself beyond a doubt; so that first point of my identity seemed fully granted.

"Sir," said I, "if I tell you my story, I must commit a friend's life to your discretion. Pass me your word it shall be sacred; and for what touches myself, I will ask no better guarantee than just your face."

He passed me his word very seriously. "But," said he "these are rather alarming prolocutions; and if there are in your story any little jostles to the law, I would beg you to bear in mind that I am a lawyer, and pass lightly."

Thereupon I told him my story from the first, he listening with his spectacles thrust up and his eyes closed, so that I sometimes feared he was asleep. But no such matter! he heard every word (as I found afterward) with such quickness of hearing and precision of memory as often surprised me. Even strange outlandish Gaelic names, heard for that time only, he remembered and would remind me of, years after. Yet when I called Alan Breck in full, we had an odd scene. The name of Alan had of course rung through Scotland, with the news of the Appin murder and the offer of the reward; and it had no sooner escaped me than the lawyer moved in his seat and opened his eyes.

"I would name no unnecessary names, Mr. Balfour," said he; "above all of Highlanders, many of whom are obnoxious to the law."

"Well, it might have been better not," said I, "but since I have let it slip, I may as well continue."

"Not at all," said Mr. Rankeillor. "I am somewhat dull of hearing, as you may have remarked; and I am far from sure I caught the name exactly. We will call your friend, if you please, Mr. Thomson — that there may be no reflections, and in future, I would take some such way with any Highlander that you may have to mention — dead or alive."

By this, I saw he must have heard the name all too clearly, and had already guessed I might be coming to the murder. If he chose to play this part of ignorance, it was no matter of mine; so I smiled, said it was no very Highland-sounding name, and consented. Through all the rest of my story Alan was Mr. Thomson; which amused me the more, as it was a piece of policy after his own heart. James Stewart, in like manner, was mentioned under the style of Mr. Thomson's kinsman; Colin Campbell passed as a Mr. Glen; and to Cluny, when I came to that part of my tale, I gave the name of "Mr. Jameson, a Highland chief." It was truly the most open farce, and I wondered that the lawyer should care to keep it up; but, after all, it was quite in the taste of that age, when there were two parties in the state, and quiet persons, with no very high opinions of their own, sought out every cranny to avoid offence to either.

"Well, well," said the lawyer, when I had quite done, "this is a great epic, a great Odyssey of yours. You must tell it, sir, in a sound Latinity when your scholarship is riper; or in English if you please, though for my part I prefer the stronger tongue. You have rolled much; QUOE REGIO IN TERRIS — what parish in Scotland (to make a homely translation) has not been filled with your wanderings? You have shown, besides, a singular aptitude for getting into false position; and yes, upon the whole, for behaving well in them. This Mr. Thomson seems to me a gentleman of some choice qualities, though perhaps a trifle bloodminded. It would please me none the worse, if (with all his merits) he were soused in the North Sea, for the man, Mr. David, is a sore embarrassment. But you are doubtless quite right to adhere to him; indubitably, he adhered to you. IT COMES — we may say — he was your true companion; nor less PARIBUS CURIS VESTIGIA FIGIT, for I dare say you would both take an orra thought upon the gallows. Well, well, these days are fortunately by; and I think (speaking humanly) that you are near the end of your troubles."

As he thus moralized on my adventures, he looked upon me with so much humour and benignity that I could scarce contain my satisfaction. I had been so long wandering with lawless people, and making my bed upon the bills and under the bare sky, that to sit once more in a clean, covered house,

157

and to talk amicably with a gentleman in broadcloth, seemed mighty elevations. Even as I thought so, my eye fell on my unseemly tatters, and I was once more plunged in confusion. But the lawyer saw and understood me. He rose, called over the stair to lay another plate, for Mr. Balfour would stay to dinner, and led me into a bedroom in the upper part of the house. Here he set before me water and soap, and a comb; and laid out some clothes that belonged to his son; and here, with another apposite tag, he left me to my toilet.

CHAPTER XXVIII
I GO IN QUEST OF MY INHERITANCE

I made what change I could in my appearance; and blithe was I to look in the glass and find the beggarman a thing of the past, and David Balfour come to life again. And yet I was ashamed of the change too, and, above all, of the borrowed clothes. When I had done, Mr. Rankeillor caught me on the stair, made me his compliments, and had me again into the cabinet.

"Sit ye down, Mr. David," said he, "and now that you are looking a little more like yourself, let me see if I can find you any news. You will be wondering, no doubt, about your father and your uncle? To be sure it is a singular tale; and the explanation is one that I blush to have to offer you. For," says he, really with embarrassment, "the matter hinges on a love affair."

"Truly," said I, "I cannot very well join that notion with my uncle."

"But your uncle, Mr. David, was not always old," replied the lawyer, "and what may perhaps surprise you more, not always ugly. He had a fine, gallant air; people stood in their doors to look after him, as he went by upon a mettle horse. I have seen it with these eyes, and I ingenuously confess not altogether without envy; for I was a plain lad myself and a plain man's son; and in those days it was a case of ODI TE, QUI BELLUS ES, SABELLE."

"It sounds like a dream," said I.

"Ay, ay," said the lawyer, "that is how it is with youth and age. Nor was that all, but he had a spirit of his own that seemed to promise great things in the future. In 1715, what must he do but run away to join the rebels? It was your father that pursued him, found him in a ditch, and brought him back MULTUM GEMENTEM; to the mirth of the whole country. However, MAJORO CANAMUS — the two lads fell in love, and that with the same lady. Mr. Ebenezer, who was the admired and the beloved, and the spoiled one, made, no doubt, mighty certain of the victory; and when he found he had deceived himself, screamed like a peacock. The whole country heard of it; how he lay sick at home, with his silly family standing round the bed in tears; now he rode from public-house to public-house, and shouted his sorrows into the lug of Tom, Dick, and Harry. Your father, Mr. David, was a kind gentleman; but he was weak, dolefully weak; took all this folly with a long countenance; and one day — by your leave! — resigned the lady. She was no such fool, however; it's from her you must inherit your excellent good sense; and she refused to be bandied from one to another. Both got upon their knees to her; and the upshot of the matter for that while was that she showed both of them the door. That was in August; dear me! the same year I came from college. The scene must have been highly farcical."

I thought myself it was a silly business, but I could not forget my father had a hand in it. "Surely, sir, it had some note of tragedy," said I.

"Why, no, sir, not at all," returned the lawyer, "for tragedy implies some ponderable matter in dispute, some DIGNUS VINDICE NODUS; and this piece of work was all about the petulance of a young ass that had been spoiled, and wanted nothing so much as to be tied up and soundly belted. However, that was not your father's view; and the end of it was, that from concession to concession on your father's part, and from one height to another of squalling sentimental selfishness upon your uncle's, they came at last to drive a sort of bargain, from whose ill-results, you have recently been smarting. The one man took the lady, the other the estate. Now, Mr. David, they talk a great deal of charity and generosity; but in his disputable state of life, I often think the happiest consequences seem to flow when a gentleman consults his lawyer and takes all the law allows him. Anyhow this piece of Quixotry on your father's part, as it was unjust in itself, has brought forth a monstruous family of injustices. Your father and mother lived and died poor folk; you were poorly reared; and in the meanwhile, what a time it has been for the tenants on the estate of Shaws! And I might add (if it was a matter I cared much about) what a time for Mr. Ebenezer!"

"And yet that is certainly the strangest part of all," said I, "that a man's nature should thus change."

"True," said Mr. Rankeillor. "And yet I imagine it was natural enough. He could not think that he had played a handsome part. Those who knew the story gave him the cold shoulder; those who knew it not, seeing one brother disappear, and the other succeed in the estate, raised a cry of murder; so that upon all sides he found himself evicted. Money was all he got by his bargain; well, he came to think the more of money. He was selfish when he was young, he is selfish now that he is old; and the latter end of all these pretty manners and fine feelings you have seen for yourself."

"Well, sir," said I, "and in all this, what is my position?"

"The estate is yours beyond a doubt," replied the lawyer. "It matters nothing what your father signed, you are the heir of entail. But your uncle is a man to fight the indefensible; and it would be likely your identity that he would call in question. A lawsuit is always expensive, and a family lawsuit always scandalous; besides which, if any of your doings with your friend Mr. Thomson were to come out, we might find that we had burned our fingers. The kindnapping, to be sure, would be a court card upon our side; if we could only prove it. But it may be difficult to prove; and my advice (upon the whole) is to make a very easy bargain with your uncle, perhaps even leaving him at Shaws where he has taken root for a quarter of a century, and contenting yourself in the meanwhile with a fair provision."

I told him I was very willing to be easy, and that to carry family concerns before the public was a step from which I was naturally much averse. In the meantime (thinking to myself) I began to see the outlines of that scheme on which we afterwards acted.

"The great affair," I asked, "is to bring home to him the kidnapping?"

"Surely," said Mr. Rankeillor, "and if possible, out of court. For make you here, Mr. David: we could no doubt find some men of the COVENANT who would swear to your reclusion; but once they were in the box, we could no longer check their testimony, and some word of your friend Mr. Thomson must certainly crop out. Which (from what you have let fall) I cannot think to be desirable."

"Well, sir," said I, "here is my way of it." And I opened my plot to him.

"But this would seem to involve my meeting the man Thomson?" says he, when I had done.

"I think so, indeed, sir," said I.

"Dear doctor!" cries he, rubbing his brow. "Dear doctor! No, Mr. David, I am afraid your scheme is inadmissible. I say nothing against your friend Mr. Thomson: I know nothing against him; and if I did — mark this, Mr. David! — it would be my duty to lay hands on him. Now I put it to you; is it wise to meet? He may have matters to his charge. He may not have told you all. His name may not be even Thomson!" cries the lawyer, twinkling; "for some of these fellows will pick up names by the roadside as another would gather laws."

"You must be the judge, sir," said I.

But it was clear my plan had taken hold upon his fancy, for he kept musing to himself till we were called to dinner and the company of Mrs. Rankeillor; and that lady had scarce left us again to ourselves and a bottle wine, here he was back harping on my proposal. When and where was I to meet my friend Mr. Thomson? Was I sure of Mr. T's discretion? Supposing we could catch the old fox tripping, would I consent to such and such a term of an agreement? — these and the like questions he kept asking at long intervals, while he thoughtfully rolled his wine upon his tongue. When I had answered all of them, seemingly to his contentment, he fell in to a still deeper muse, even the claret being now forgotten. Then he got a sheet of paper and a pencil, and set to work writing and weighing every word; and at last touched a bell and had his clerk into the chamber.

"Torrance," said he, "I must have this written out fair against to-night; and when it is done, you will be so kind as put to on your hat and be ready to come along with this gentleman and me, for you will probably be wanted as a witness."

"What, sir," cried I, as soon as the clerk was gone, "are you to venture it?"

"Why, so it would appear," says he, filling his glass. "But let us speak no more of business. The very sight of Torrance brings in my head a little droll matter of some years ago, when I had made a tryst with the poor oaf at the cross of Edinburgh. Each had gone his proper errand; and when it came four o'clock Torrance had been taking a glass and did not know his master, and I, who had forgot my spectacles, was so blind without them, that I give you my word I did not know my own clerk." And thereupon he laughed heartily.

I said it was an odd chance, and smiled out of politeness; but what held me all the afternoon in wonder, he kept returning and dwelling on this story, and telling it again with fresh details and laughter; so that I began at last to be quite put out of countenance and feel ashamed of my friend's folly.

Towards the time I had appointed with Alan, we set out from the house, Mr. Rankeillor and I arm in arm, and Torrance following behind with the deed in his pocket and a covered basket in his hand. All through the town, the lawyer was bowing right and left, and continually being button-holed by gentlemen on maters of burgh or private business; and I could see he was one greatly looked up to in the county. At last we were clear of the houses, and began to go along the side of the haven and towards the Hawes Inn and the ferry pier, the scene of my misfortune. I could not look upon the place without emotion, recalling how many that had been there with me that day were now no more: Ransome taken, I could hope, from the evil to come; Shuan passed when I dared not follow him; and the poor souls that had gone down with the brig in her last plunge. All these, and the brig herself, I had outlived; and come through these hardships and fearful perils without scathe. My only thought should have been of gratitude; and yet I could not behold the place without sorrow for others and a chill of recollected fear.

I was so thinking when, upon a sudden, Mr. Rankeillor cried out, clapped his hand to his pockets, and began to laugh.

"Why," he cries, "if this be not a farcical adventure? After all that I said, I have forgot my glasses!"

At that, of course, I understood the purpose of his anecdote, and knew that if he had left his spectacles at home, it had been done on purpose, so that he might have the benefit of Alan's help without the awkwardness of recognizing him. And indeed it was well thought upon; for now (suppose things to go the very worst) how could Rankeillor swear to my friend's identity, or how be made to bear damaging evidence against myself? For all that, he had been a long while of finding out his want, and had spoken to and recognized a good few persons as we came through the town; and I had little doubt myself that he saw reasonably well.

As soon as we were past the Hawes (where I recognized the landlord smoking his pipe in the door, and was amazed to see him look no older) Mr. Rankeillor changed the order of march, walking behind with Torrance and sending me forward in the manner of a scout. I went up the hill, whistling from time to time my Gaelic air; and at lenght I had the pleasure to hear it answered and to see Alan rise from behind a bush. He was somewhat dashed in spirits, having passed a long day alone skulking in the county, and made but a poor meal in an alehouse near Dundas. But at the mere sight of my clothes, he began to brighten up; and as soon as I had told him in what a forward state our matters were, and the part I looked to him to play in what remained, he sprang into a new man.

"And that is a very good notion of yours," says he; "and I dare to say that you could lay your hands upon no better man to put it through than Alan Breck. It is not a thing (mark ye) that any one could do, but takes a gentleman of penetration. But it sticks in my head your lawyer-man will be somewhat wearying to see me," says Alan.

Accordingly I cried and waved on Mr. Rankeillor, who came up alone and was presented to my friend Mr. Thomson.

"Mr. Thomson, I am pleased to meet you," said he. "But I have forgotten my glasses; and our friend, Mr. David here," (clapping me on the shoulder) "will tell you that I am little better than blind, and that you must not be surprised if I pass you by to-morrow."

This he said, thinking that Alan would be pleased; but the Highlandman's vanity was ready to startle at a less matter than that.

"Why, sir," says he stiffly, "I would say it mattered the less as we are met here for a particular end, to see justice done to Mr. Balfour, and by what I can see, not very likely to have much else in common. But I accept your apology, which was a very proper one to make."

"And that is more than I could look for, Mr. Thomson," said Rankeillor heartily. "And now as you and I are the chief actors in this enterprise, I think we should come into a nice agreement; to which end, I propose that you should lend me your arm, for (what with the dusk and the want of my glasses) I am not very clear as to the path; and as for you, Mr. David, you will find Torrance a pleasant kind of body to speak with. Only let me remind you, it's quite needless he should hear more of your adventures or those of — ahem — Mr. Thomson."

Accordingly these two went on ahead in very close talk, and Torrance and I brought up the rear.

Night was quite come when we came in view of the house of Shaws. Ten had been gone some time; it was dark and mild, with a pleasant rustling wind in the south-west that covered the sound of our approach; and as we drew near we saw no glimmer of light in any portion of the building. It seemed my uncle was already in bed, which was indeed the best thing for our arrangements. We made our last whispered consultations some fifty yards away; and then the lawyer and Torrance and I crept quietly up and crouched down beside the corner of the house; and as soon as we were in our places, Alan strode to the door without concealment and began to knock.

CHAPTER XXIX

I COME INTO MY KINGDOM

For some time Alan volleyed upon the door, and his knocking only roused the echoes of the house and neighbourhood. At last, however, I could hear the noise of a window gently thrust up, and knew that my uncle had come to his observatory. By what light there was, he would see Alan standing, like a dark shadow, on the steps; the three witnesses were hidden quite out of his view; so that there was nothing to alarm an honest man in his own house. For all that, he studied his visitor awhile in silence, and when he spoke his voice had a quaver of misgiving.

"What's this?" says he. "This is nae kind of time of night for decent folk; and I have nae dealings wi' nighthawks. What brings ye here? I have a blunderbuss."

"Is that yoursel', Mr. Balfour?" returned Alan, stepping back and looking up into the darkness. "Have a care of that blunderbuss; they're nasty things to burst."

"What brings ye here? and whae are ye?" says my uncle angrily.

"I have no manner of inclination to rowt out my name to the countryside," said Alan; "but what brings me here is another story, being more of your affairs than mine; and if ye're sure it's what ye would like, I'll set it to a tune and sing to you."

"And what is't?" asked my uncle.

"David," says Alan,

"What was that?" cried my uncle, in a mighty changed voice.

"Shall I give ye the rest of the name, then?" said Alan.

There was a pause; and then, "I'm thinking I'll better let ye in," says my uncle doubtfully.

"I dare say that," said Alan;" but the point is, would I go? Now I will tell you what I am thinking. I am thinking that it is here upon this doorstep that we must confer upon this business; and it shall be here or nowhere at all whatever; for I would have you to understand that I am as stiffnecked as yoursel', and a gentleman of better family."

This change of note disconcerted Ebenezer; he was a little while digesting it, and then says he, "Weel, weel, what must be must," and shut the window. But it took him a long time to get downstairs, and a little longer to undo the fastenings, repenting (I dare say) and taken with fresh claps of fear at every second step and every bolt and bar. At last, however, we heard the creak of the hinges, and its seems my uncle slipped gingerly out and (seeing that Alan had stepped back a pace or two) sat him down on the top doorstep with the blunderbuss ready in his hands.

"And now," said he, "mind I have my blunderbuss, and if ye take a step nearer ye're as good as deid."

"And a very civil speech," says Alan, "to be sure."

"Na," says my uncle, "but this is no a very chancy kind of a proceeding, and I'm bound to be prepared. And now that we understand each other, ye'll can name your business."

"Why," says Alan, "you that are a man of so much understanding, will doubtless have perceived that I am a Hieland gentleman. My name has nae business in my story; but the county of my friends is no very far from the Isle of Mull, of which ye will have heard. It seems there was a ship lost in those parts; and the next day a gentleman of my family was seeking wreck-wood for his fire along the sands, when he came upon a lad that was halfdrowned. Well, he brought him to: and he and some other gentlemen took and clapped him in an auld, ruined castle, where from that day to this he has been a great expense to my friends. My friends are a wee wildlike, and not so particular about the law as some that I could name; and finding that the lad owned some decent folk, and was your born nephew, Mr. Balfour, they asked me to give ye a bit call and to confer upon the matter. And I may tell ye at the off-go, unless we can agree upon some terms, ye are little likely to set eyes upon him. For my friends," added Alan simply, "are no very well off."

My uncle cleared his throat. "I'm no very caring," says he. "He wasnae a good lad at the best of it, and I've nae call to interfere."

"Ay, ay," said Alan, "I see what ye would be at: pretending ye don't care, to make the ransom smaller."

"Na," said my uncle, "it's the mere truth. I take nae matter of interest in the lad, and I'll pay nae ransom, and ye can make a kirk and mill of him for what I care."

"Hoot, sir," says Alan. "Blood's thicker than water, in the deil's name! Ye cannae desert your brother's son for the fair shame of it; and if ye did, and it came to be kent, ye wouldnae be very popular in your countryside, or I'm the more deceived."

"I'm no just very popular the way it is," returned Ebenezer; and I dinnae see how it would come to be kent. No by me, onyway; nor yet by you or your friends. So that's idle talk, my buckie," says he.

"Then it'll have to be David that tells it," said Alan.

"How's that?" says my uncle, sharply.

"Ou, just this way," says Alan. "My friends would doubtless keep your nephew as long as there was any likelihood of siller to be made of it, but if there was nane, I am clearly of opinion they would let him gang where he pleased, and be damned to him!"

"Ay, but I'm no very caring about that either," said my uncle. "I wouldnae be muckle made up with that."

"I was thinking that," said Alan.

"And what for why?" asked Ebenezer.

"Why, Mr. Balfour," replied Alan, "by all that I could hear, there were two ways of it: either ye liked David and would pay to get him back; or else ye had very good reasons for not wanting him, and would pay for us to keep him. It seems it's no the first; well then, it's the second; and blithe am I to ken it, for it should be a pretty penny in my pocket and the pockets of my friends."

"I dinnae follow ye there," said my uncle.

"No?" said Alan. "Well, see here: you dinnae want the lad back; well what do ye want done with him, and how much will ye pay?"

My uncle made no answer, but shifted uneasily on his seat.

"Come, sir," cried Alan. "I would have ye to ken that I am a gentleman: I bear a king's name: I am nae rider to kick my shanks at your hall door. Either give me an answer in civility, and that out of hand; or by the top of Glencoe, I will ram three feet of iron through your vitals."

"Eh, man," cried my uncle, scrambling to his feet, "give me a meenit! What's like wrong with ye? I'm just a plain man an nae dancing master; and I'm trying to be as ceevil as it's morally possible. As for that wild talk, it's fair disreputable. Vitals, says you! And where would I be with my blunderbuss?" he snarled.

"Power and your auld hands are but as the snail to the swallow against the bright steel in the hands of Alan," said the other. "Before your jottering finger could find the trigger, the hilt would dirl on your breast bone."

"Eh, man, whae's denying it?" said my uncle. "Pit it as please, hae't your ain way; I'll do naething to cross ye. Just tell me what like ye'll be wanting, and ye'll see that we'll can agree fine."

"Troth, sir," said Alan, "I ask for nothing but plain dealing. In two words: do ye want the lad killed or kept?"

"O, sirs!" cried Ebenezer. "O, sirs, me! that's no kind of language!"

"Killed or kept?" repeated Alan.

"O keepit, keepit !" wailed my uncle. "We'll have nae bloodshed, if you please."

"Well," says Alan, "as ye please; that'll be the dearer."

"The dearer?" cries Ebenezer. "Would ye syle your hands wi' crime?"

"Hoot !" said Alan, "they're baith crime, whatever ! And the killing's easier, and quicker, and surer. Keeping the lad'll be a fashous job, a fashous, kittle business.

"I'll have him keep it, though," returned my uncle. "I never had naething to do with onything morally wrong; and I'm no gaun to begin to pleasure a wild Hielandman."

"Ye're unco scrupulous," sneered Alan.

I'm a man o' principle," said Ebenezer simply; and if I have to pay for it, I'll have to pay for it. And besides," says he, "ye forget the lad's my brother's son."

"Well, well," said Alan, "and now about the price. It's no very easy for me to set a name upon it; I would first have to ken some small matters. I would have to ken, for instance, what ye gave Hoseason at the first off-go?"

"Hoseason !" cries my uncle, struck aback, "what for?"

"For kidnapping David," says Alan.

"It's a lee, it's a black lee!" cried my uncle. "He was never kidnapped. He lee'd in his throat that tauld ye that. Kidnapped? He never was !"

"That's no fault of mine, nor yet of yours," said Alan; "nor yet of Hoseason's if he's man that can be trusted."

"What do ye mean?" cried Ebenezer. "Did Hoseason tell ye ?"

"Why, ye donnered auld runt, how else would I ken?" cried Alan. "Hoseason and me are partners; we gang shares; so ye can see for yoursel's what good ye can do leeing. And I must plainly say ye drove a fool's bargain when ye let a man like the sailor-man so far forward in your private matters. But that's past praying for, and ye must lie on your bed the way ye made it. And the point in hand is just this: what did ye pay him?"

"Has he tauld ye himsel'?" asked my uncle.

"That's my concern," said Alan.

"Weel," said my uncle. "I dinnae care what he said he lee'd, and the solemn God's truth is this, that I gave him twenty pound. But I'll be perfec'ly honest with ye: forby that, he was to have the selling of the lad in Caroliny, which would be as muckle mair, but no from my pocket, ye see."

"Thank you, Mr. Thomson. That will do excellently well," said the lawyer, stepping forward; and then mighty civilly, "Good evening. Mr. Balfour," said he.

And, "Good evening, Uncle Ebenezer," said I.

And, "It's a braw night, Mr. Balfour," added Torrance.

Never a word said my uncle, neither black nor white; but just sat where he was on the top doorstep hands tared upon us like a man turned to stone. Alan filched away his blunderbuss; and the lawyer, taking him by the arm, plucked him up from the doorstep, led him into the kitchen, whither we all followed, and set him down in a chair beside the hearth, where the fire was out and only a rushlight burning.

There we all looked upon him for a while, exulting greatly in our success, but yet with a sort of pity for the man's shame.

"Come, come, Mr. Ebenezer," said the lawyer, "you must not be down-hearted, for I promise you we shall make easy terms. In the meanwhile give us the cellar key, and Torrance shall draw us a bottle of your father's wine in honour of the event." Then, turning to me and taking me by the hand, "Mr. David," says he, "I wish you all joy in your good fortune, which I believe to be deserved." And then to Alan, with a spice of drollery, "Mr. Thomson, I pay you my compliment; it was most artfully conducted; but in one point you somewhat outran my comprehension. Do I understand your name to be James? or Charles? Or is it George, perhaps?"

"And why should it be any of the three, sir?" quoth Alan, drawing himself up, like one who smelt an offence.

"Only, sir, that you mentioned a king's name," replied Rankeillor; "and as there has never yet been a King Thomson, or his fame at least has never come my way, I judged you must refer to that you had in baptism."

This was just the stab that Alan would feel keenest, and I am free to confess he took it very ill. Not a word would he answer, but stepped off to the far end of the kitchen, and sat down and sulked; and it was not till I stepped after him, and gave him my hand, and thanked him by title as the chief spring of my success, that he began to smile a bit, and was at last prevailed upon to join our party.

By that time we had the fire lighted, and a bottle of wine uncorked; a good supper came out of the basket, to which Torrance and I and Alan set ourselves down; while the lawyer and my uncle passed into the next chamber to consult. They stayed there closeted about an hour; at the end of which period they had come to a good understanding, and my uncle and I set our hands to the agreement in a formal manner. By the terms of this, my uncle bound himself to satisfy Rankeillor as to his intromissions, and to pay me two clear thirds of the yearly income of Shaws.

So the beggar in the ballad had come home; and when I lay down that night on the kitchen chests, I was a man of means and had a name in the country. Alan and Torrance and Rankeillor slept and snored on their hard beds; but for me who had lain out under heaven and upon dirt and stones, so many days and nights, and often with an empty belly, and in fear of death, this good change in my case unmanned me more than any of the former evil ones; and I lay till dawn, looking at the fire on the roof and planning the future.

CHAPTER XXX

GOOD-BYE!

So far as I was concerned myself, I had come to port; but I had still Alan, to whom I was so much beholden, on my hands; and I felt besides a heavy charge in the matter of the murder and James of the Glens. On both these heads I unbosomed to Rankeillor the next morning, walking to and fro about six of the clock before the house of Shaws, and with nothing in view but the fields and woods that had been my ancestors' and were now mine. Even as I spoke on these grave subjects, my eye would take a glad bit of a run over the prospect, and my heart jump with pride.

About my clear duty to my friend, the lawyer had no doubt, I must help him out of the country at whatever risk; but in the case of James, he was of a different mind.

"Mr. Thomson," says he, "is one thing, Mr. Thomson's kinsman quite another. I know little of the facts, but I gather that a great noble (whom we will call, if you like, the Duke of Argyll) has some concern and is even supposed to feel some animosity in the matter. The D. of A. is doubtless an excellent nobleman; but, Mr. David, TIMEO QUI NOCUERE DEOS. If you interfere to baulk his vengeance, you should remember there is one was to shut your testimony out; and that is to put you in the dock. There, you would be in the same pickle as Mr. Thomson's kinsman. You will object that you are innocent; well, but so is he. And to be tried for your life before a Highland jury, on a Highland quarrel and with a Highland judge upon the bench, would be a brief transition to the gallows."

Now I had made all these reasonings before and found no very good reply to them; so I put on all the simplicity I could. "In that case, sir," said I, "I would just have to be hanged — would I not?"

"Me dear boy," cries he, "go in God's name, and do what you think is right. It is a poor thought that at my time of life I should be advising you to choose the safe and shameful; and I take it back with an apology. Go and do your duty; and be hanged, if you must, like a gentleman. There are worse things in the world than to be hanged."

"Not many, sir," said I, smiling.

"Why, yes, sir," he cried, "very many. And it would be ten times better for your uncle (to go no farther afield) if he were dangling decently upon a gibbet."

Thereupon he turned into the house (still in a great fervour of mind, so that I saw I had pleased him heartily) and there he wrote me two letters, making his comments on them as he wrote.

"This," says he, "is to my bankers, the British Linen Company, placing a credit to your name. Consult Mr. Thomson, he will know of ways; and you, with this credit, can supply the means. I trust you will be a good husband of your money; but in the afair of a friend like Mr. Thomson, I would be even prodigal. Then for his kinsman there is no better way than that you should seek the Advocate, tell him your tale and offer testimony ; whether he may take it or not, is quite another matter, and will turn on the D. of A. Now that you may reach the Lord Advocate well recommended, I give you here a letter to a namesake of your own, the learned Mr. Balfour of Pilrig, a man whom I esteem. It will look better that you should be presented by one of your own name; and the laird of Pilrig is much looked up to in the Faculty and stands well with Lord Advocate Grant. I would not trouble him, if I were you, with any particulars; and (do you know?) I think it would be needless to refer to Mr. Thomson. Form yourself upon the laird, he's a good model; when you deal with the Advocate, be discreet; and in all these matters, may the Lord guide you, Mr. David!"

Thereupon he took his farewell, and set out with Torrance for the Ferry, while Alan and I turned our faces to the city of Edinburgh. As we went by the footpath and besides the gateposts and the unfinished lodge, we kept looking back at the house of my fathers. It stood there, bare and great and smokeless, like a place not lived in; only in one of the top windows, there was the peak of the nightcap bobbing up and down and back and forward, like the head of a rabbit from a burrow. I had little welcome when I came, and less kindness while I stayed, but at least I was watched as I went away.

Alan and I went slowly forward upon our way, having little heart either to walk or speak. The same thought was uppermost in both, that we were near the time of our parting and remembrance of all the bygone days sat upon us sorely. We talked indeed of what should be done; and it was resolved that Alan should keep to the country, biding now here, now there, but coming once in the day to a particular place where I might be able to communicate with him, either in my own person or by messenger. In the meanwhile I was to seek out a lawyer, who was an Appin Stewart, and a man therefore to be wholly trusted; and it should be his part to find a ship and to arrange for Alan's safe embarkation. No sooner was this business done, than the words seemed to leave us; and though I would seek to jest with Alan, under the name of Mr. Thomson, and he with me on my new clothes and my estate, you could feel very well that we were nearer tears than laughter.

We came the by-way over the hill of Corstorphine; and when we got near to the place called Rest-and-be-Thankful, and looked down on Corstorphine bogs and over to the city and the castle on the hill, we both stopped, for we both knew without a word said that we had come to where our ways parted. Here he repeated to me once again what had been agreed upon between us; the address of the lawyer, the daily hour at which Alan might be found, and the signals that were to be made by any that came seeking him. Then I gave what money I had (a guinea or two of Rankeillor's) so that he should not starve in the meanwhile; and we stood a space, and looked over at Edinburgh in silence.

"Well, good-bye," said Alan, and held out his left hand.

"Good-bye," said I, and gave the hand a little grasp and went off downhill.

Neither one of us looked the other in the face, nor so long as he was in my view did I take one back glance at the friend I was leaving. But as I went on my way to the city, I felt so lost and lonesome, that I could have found it in my heart to sit down by the dyke, and cry and weep like any baby.

It was coming near noon when I passed in by the West Kirk and the Grassmarket into the streets of the capital. The huge height of the buildings, running up to ten and fifteen storeys, the narrow arched entries that continually vomited passengers, the wares of the merchants in their windows, the hubbub and endless stir, the foul smells and the fine clothes, and a hundred other particulars too small to mention, struck me into a kind of stupor of surprise, so that I let the crowd carry me to and fro; and yet all the time what I was thinking of was Alan at Rest-and-be-Thankful; and all the time (although you would think I would not choose but be delighted with these braws and novelties) there was a cold gnawing in my inside like a remorse for something wrong.

The hand of Providence brought me in my drifting to the very doors of the British Linen Company's bank.

THE END

OTHER TITLES IN THIS SERIES

Printed in Hungary